Heartless Rebel

LAURIE LONDON

Previously published as Rebel's Desire © 2015, Laurie London

Copyright © 2024 by Laurie London

All rights reserved.

Edited by Kim Nadelson and Megan Stevens

Cover design, interior design and map by Laurie London

Ebook Edition: 978-0-9882734-6-7

Print Edition: 9780988273474

No part of this book may be reproduced in any form or by any electronic or mechanical means, including information storage and retrieval systems, without written permission from the author, except for the use of brief quotations in a book review.

This is a work of fiction. Names, characters, places and incidents are the product of the author's imagination or are used fictitiously. Any resemblance to actual persons, living, dead, or undead, is purely coincidental.

PRAISE FOR LAURIE LONDON

"Paranormal romance gets a sexy addition with London's sizzling series debut." Publishers Weekly on Bonded By Blood

Finalist (as Assassin's Touch), National Romance Fiction Award

"Fiery action and romance make (Dark Assassin) a Winner! – Joyfully Reviewed

"Ms. London's world of Iron Portal is indeed enthralling. She again brought in an alpha hero to swoon over and a love story to sigh over."
– Under the Covers Book Blog

For sneak peeks, exclusives, sale notices and goodies, subscribe to Laurie's mailing list:
http://laurielondonbooks.com/mailing-list-sign-up/

OTHER BOOKS BY LAURIE LONDON

IRON PORTAL SERIES

Dark Assassin

Midnight Rogue

Hidden Warrior

Heartless Rebel

SWEETBLOOD WORLD

Bonded By Blood

Embraced By Blood

Tempted By Blood

Seduced By Blood

Hidden By Blood

Enticed By Blood

Unraveled By Blood

Enchanted By Blood

NOCTURNE FALLS UNIVERSE

How Knot to Marry a Vampire

A NOTE FROM THE AUTHOR

The following map is a fictional interpretation of Washington State after a big earthquake that occurred years ago in this story. I took a lot of creative license and used the actual map only as a starting point. You'll notice that coastlines, mountain ranges, islands and other elements are not exactly how they look today.

If you live here, like I do, and your area isn't depicted correctly, that's because it was destroyed by the earthquake…or it's underwater. Sorry.

IRON PORTAL REALMS
BALKIRK
BRITISH COLUMBIA
CLUCK ISLAND
MOUNT PILCHUCK
VALLENBERG
GRANITE FALLS
THE INSTITUTE
GREENWAY
CRESTENFAHL
CRYSTAL PEAK STATION
RED MOUNTAIN
HOT
NEW SEATTLE
SUMMER'S FOLLY
RECKLESS MOTORSPORTS
ROSEVILLE
CASCADIA
(BARROWLANDS)
IRON HAVEN
PACIFICA
DERRY'S FOLLY
PORTLAND

CHAPTER ONE

If Keely Weber hadn't been in such a hurry to get back to the shop, she would've noticed the crowd gathered on the corner of First and Yesler and gone a different way.

In fact, she didn't figure out it was an organized group and not just a bunch of people rushing home from work on a Friday afternoon until she was smack-dab in the middle and being jostled from side to side.

She hated being buffeted around like this but refrained from doing anything other than hunching her shoulders and tucking her hands deeper into the front pocket of her hoodie. She couldn't be late with the money. Her sister would be waiting for her, and Becca wasn't exactly patient.

"'Scuse me," she mumbled, pulling out her earbuds.

That's when she heard the chanting.

"Abominations."

Clap clap clap.

"Satan's spawn."

Clap clap clap.

"Stop the lies."

Her stomach twisted into knots, and a familiar revulsion rushed through her.

Protesters. She should've known. After all, this was the edge of the Circus District, a seedy part of New Seattle that was home to individuals with special ability Talents—either real or faked.

Davin Reaux, a powerful but shady businessman with high-up ties in the government, made sure the army turned a blind eye to this area of the city near the shipyards. He wasn't always successful—there were still the occasional raids where the army came in and rounded up Talents they thought they could use in the war against Cascadia, a world hidden beyond secret portals whose barbarian people came over here to wreak havoc. They were responsible for random bombings and the deaths of innocent people.

But, for the most part, the army left the Circus District alone. Fueled, Keely was sure, by the hush money that small businesses like hers and Becca's paid to Mr. Reaux each and every month.

Money that would be late if she didn't make it back to the shop soon.

Keely spun around, looking for a way out of the

crowd, but dozens of bodies pressed in around her. If anyone recognized her…

At least it had been drizzling lightly when she left the bank, so her hoodie was up, her long auburn hair covered.

"Aberration."

"Mistake."

"You're not welcome here."

The hateful words gnawed at her.

At one time, she'd been just like these people. Clutching her father's hand, she'd held signs and shouted words. Words she didn't fully understand.

Before his show became one of the most-watched channels on the Internet.

Before her Talent and Becca's had manifested and they were kicked out of the house.

A man who preached that Talents were possessed by demons couldn't exactly have two of them living under his roof, now could he? It wasn't good for business.

She hated that people hated her for something she couldn't change. Something she didn't ask for. It was one thing if someone judged her because of her tattoos and piercings. Those were choices she'd consciously made. Most of them, that is. But being born a Talent? Yeah, right. As if she'd ever in a million years choose to be a freak.

Careful not to disturb the bandage covering her new tattoo, she shoved her hands up the opposite sleeves of her sweatshirt and dug her fingernails into her skin. She imagined the ten half-moon indentations she was making and welcomed the pain. It gave her clarity. Helped her focus.

Spotting a gap in the crowd, she turned to the side and shouldered her way through the people.

There. She was on the open sidewalk again. She breathed a sigh of relief.

If she hurried, she could make it back to the shop with a few minutes to spare. To say she was glad she hadn't stopped at the street vendor selling coconut cream pie bites was an understatement. Those little desserts were a major weakness of hers, and the line had been short. But if she had stopped, she'd be running even later than she already was. Plus, Becca would've smelled the toasted coconut on her breath and flipped out that Keely hadn't come straight back to the shop with all this money in her pocket. Caving to temptation seriously wasn't worth her sister's wrath.

A hand clamped around her upper arm, the one with the new tattoo, and jerked her around.

She hissed in pain. "Hey, let g—"

Someone yanked down her hoodie, and a few people gasped. Glancing around the group, she cursed under her breath at her colossal bad luck.

A sandy-haired guy in a T-shirt that said "Don't Be Fooled" stood in front of her, staring her up and down with no attempt to disguise the disgust on his face. "Keely Weber. I thought that was you."

"Hey, Cole." It was hard to believe that at one time back in high school, she'd actually had a crush on him, thought he was hot. Funny how when someone's a jerk, they're suddenly as ugly on the outside as they are on the inside. "You're looking…as righteous as ever."

Satisfaction flared momentarily in his eyes and the word *thanks* began to form on his lips before he realized she hadn't meant it as a compliment.

Psych!

"What happened to you?" a young woman asked. She was rocking a baby in her arms, but the movement looked more like a nervous tic than infant-soothing. "You used to be so…so normal."

Keely shrugged. "What can I say, Robin? Getting kicked out of the house and shunned by family and friends tends to change a person."

Cole muttered something under his breath to the guy next to him who laughed. Unlike the seven or eight people in the crowd she recognized, he didn't look familiar.

"What was that, Cole?" she asked sweetly. "Speak up."

The group seemed to be closing in around her. Keely really should stop goading them, but she couldn't help herself. It was like poking a hornets' nest with a stick.

Cole looked her straight in the eye. "I said, *and not for the better.*"

She balled her hands into tight fists, wanting nothing more than to punch him right in the mouth. Then she'd donkey-kick the pimply guy behind her, roundhouse-kick the guy to her left who laughed like a horse, and elbow the skinny chick to her right who kept nodding. And if Robin put her baby down, she'd donkey-kick her, too.

A girl could dream, couldn't she?

She couldn't believe she used to be friends with some of these people.

Somebody shoved her from behind, sending her stumbling in Cole's direction, but he stepped aside with the grace of a prizefighter. She fell to her knees, catching herself at the last minute with her hands, but as she did so, the bank envelope flipped out of her sweatshirt pocket and skidded along the ground.

She dove for it, but she wasn't fast enough.

Cole scooped it up, peered inside and whistled. He elbowed the guy next to him. "Yo, check it out."

"Whoa," his friend said. "I thought everyone paid in credits now. Who even takes real money anymore?"

She rose to her feet. This couldn't be happening. Please let this be a bad dream. "Give that to me. It doesn't belong to you."

"What is this?" Cole taunted, holding it just out of reach. "Blood money?"

If she weren't so freaked out, she would've laughed. This suburban boy living in a gated community with private security and a monthly allowance from daddy had no clue what that even meant. He'd probably heard it in a movie and thought it sounded edgy.

"Cole, please. I need that."

"What's it for?"

None of your damn business.

She ground her teeth together, trying to hold her patience in check. "It's to pay a bill. A very important one."

As if on cue, the old clock in Pioneer Square began to chime. It was the top of the hour. Time had officially run out.

Panic surged through her like a drug. She stood on her tiptoes to see if she could spot the shiny black limousine heading toward the shop, but there were too many people crowding around her.

What would Mr. Reaux do if the payment was late? She'd heard stories about broken arms and hostage-taking. Everyone in the District had.

"A bill, huh?" Cole grinned. He wasn't about to hand it over.

She lunged at the envelope and actually touched it, but Cole jerked it out of the way and the bills went flying.

"Noooo!"

The crowd surged forward, arms and hands scrabbling in the air.

Although she managed to snatch a few bills from

people, it wasn't nearly all of it, and the crowd quickly dispersed, leaving her on her hands and knees in the middle of the sidewalk.

Cole tossed a smile over his shoulder as he strolled away. "Thanks for your generous donation to the cause. Loser."

"Screw you!" Keely shouted.

She pushed herself up, her hands and knees shaking. How had she lost all that money? What was she going to do now? Becca was going to kill her. Seriously kill her. That was more than a week's income for the shop.

She'd never met Mr. Reaux before. He always waited out in the car when one of his men came inside to collect. But she was late. Would his car still be idling at the curb out front or would he come back later? She thought again about what would happen if he didn't get his money and hoped to God those rumors weren't true. Could they skip this month and pay twice as much next month?

When Keely got back to Sisters Books and Fortunes, she had her answer.

The door was unlocked, and Becca was gone.

Toryn Flynn ran a cloth over the blade of his knife and wished he were cleaning off the blood of his enemies.

The night was a bust—which seemed to come as a

complete surprise to everyone. Everyone, that is, except him. Maybe the other Iron Guild warriors didn't have a problem relying on intel from someone who'd betrayed them in the past, but he sure as hell did.

The sky to the east, above the Cascade Mountains where the portal he'd come through was located, was inky black. Sunrise was still a long way off. Whoever said time stands still for no man had clearly never been on a stakeout.

"Damn," Sean said, shaking his head as if he believed his own bullshit. "I thought for sure he would show tonight."

Aye, I'll bet you did.

Their target, Davin Reaux, was the head of a powerful organized crime ring and responsible for financing deadly raids into Cascadia. Unless they took the bloke out, Cascadians would continue to be in danger. Just recently, a raid that *Sean* had taken part in had killed several innocent Cascadians and shaken their entire region.

"I'm sure he'll show up." Vince, the newest member of the Iron Guild, kept his binoculars trained on the road below them.

Toryn made a sound of disgust, sheathed the knife and strode to another area of the parking garage roof. Sean was a Tracker-Talent—if anyone should know how to find the bastard, he should. So the fact that he couldn't was just another red flag.

Until recently, Vince and Sean had been imprisoned together by the Pacifican army. For ten years, Vince refused to divulge the location of a secret portal—a decision that saved many innocent Cascadian lives, branded him a hero, and secured him a place on their elite team of warriors.

But Sean? At the first chance he got, he'd helped the enemy on their mission into Cascadia.

Toryn didn't trust him. Not by a long shot.

He leaned against the cement barrier and looked out over the city. Street noises wafted up the six stories. The forlorn sound of a boat horn echoed from somewhere out on the dark bay. To the north, the Old Space Needle lit up the night. Although still the city's iconic symbol, it had been damaged by a massive earthquake many years ago and was no longer safe inside.

Footsteps shuffled behind him, then a bottle of Irish whiskey was thrust in front of him.

"Here." It was his best friend, Konal. "Need some liquid patience?"

"Patience isn't my problem." Toryn grabbed the bottle and knocked back a huge swig. The alcohol burned a welcome path down his throat.

"Says the guy who never relaxes." Konal jerked his chin at the street below. "Maybe you need to pay a visit to one of the shops for a massage *and* a happy ending."

"The thing I don't understand is why everyone's so willing to trust what the Professor says," Toryn said, using Sean's prison nickname. As far as he was concerned, betrayal was the ultimate trust-killer.

"Because without his intel," Konal replied, "we wouldn't have known who funded the last raid into Cascadia."

"Don't you find it a wee bit convenient that we got here only to find that the club employs a couple of Psychic-Talent bouncers?" Toryn growled. "So we're forced to wait for the bloke and hope that he shows up sometime in the next millennia."

Their original plan had been to wait inside Aphrodistic, a strip club that Reaux owned. Asher and Konal were going to scope out the place first and the rest of them would have followed a few minutes later. But when the first two warriors got to the front of the line, everything went south. One of the thug bouncers turned out to be a Psychic-Talent and came after them, wielding a knife and a really bad attitude.

Depending on how much the Talent had been able to sense, Reaux could very well know that warriors from Cascadia were after him, and he was probably, at this very moment, making arrangements to protect himself even further.

How bloody convenient was that?

Konal grabbed the bottle from Toryn, took a swig and wiped his mouth with the back of his hand. "What's not to love about an excuse to drink with the lads?"

The *lads*? So Konal trusted the Professor, too. He shoved past his friend.

"Where are you going?"

"I need some air."

When would these guys realize that you couldn't blindly put your faith in someone who wanted something in return? In the Professor's case, his motives were clear. He wanted out of the jail pit, so he was willing to say and do anything to accomplish that. But with some people, their agendas weren't so obvious. Not until you risked everything only to be betrayed in return.

Toryn had just made it to street level when an entourage of black Town Cars sped past, heading in the direction of the club.

Could it be Reaux?

He sprinted down the street just in time to see three vehicles turn the corner toward Aphrodistic. The neon arrow pointing the way originally advertised a gentlemen's club, only some of the letters had been busted out, so now it read *A Gentle Club*.

If he hurried, he might be able to see who got out of the cars. If it were Reaux, he'd rush the guy and take him out. Bodyguards be damned. But he hadn't gotten more than a few steps from the alley when he heard shouts.

Rival gangs? A turf war? He sure as hell didn't want to get involved in that.

He hesitated as a small hooded figure darted around

the corner and headed straight for him. Based on the curves, he guessed a woman. Toryn saw a flash of red hair as she threw a glance behind her.

It looked as if she was running away from someone or something, but he didn't see any pursuers.

However, if Reaux's men were onto the warriors, this could be a trap, designed to flush them out. He reached inside his leather jacket and touched the hilt of his blade.

When she was ten feet away, her eyes locked onto his. The panic in her expression was very real, but it quickly turned into determination. She tore off her sweatshirt, threw it behind a trashcan and flung herself into his arms.

"What the bloody hell, woman?"

Her whole body pressed against his. She was soft. And very voluptuous.

"Work with me," she whispered. "Please."

Then she pulled his head close and kissed him.

CHAPTER TWO

Keely needed to sell this kiss.

She gave it everything she had, which wasn't too hard given that the stranger she was kissing was smoking hot.

With her mouth pressed to his, she ran her hands up the muscular plane of his chest, over his leather jacket, and wrapped her arms around his neck. He tasted and smelled amazing—like whiskey and mint, one hundred percent male. She'd always been impulsive, but she'd never done anything quite like this before.

At first his mouth had been rigid, but then his lips softened and began to move against hers, his hand slipped into her hair. The guy was actually kissing her back!

Good. It made this all the more believable.

All she had to do was make it seem like *she* wasn't the

woman her pursuers were after. *That* woman had been alone and wearing a faded grey sweatshirt with the hood pulled up. *This* woman wore a blue tank top, had longish red hair that fell past her shoulders, and was engaging in some serious PDA with her boyfriend.

Two totally different people, right? God, she hoped so.

From the corner of her eye, she saw her two pursuers sprint around the corner. They were coming right this way.

For a moment she questioned her split-second decision to stop running and try outsmarting them. She was desperate. She just hoped she hadn't been *too* desperate.

After discovering that Becca was missing, Keely had gone from shop to shop, trying to find someone who knew what had happened, but no one had wanted to talk. It was as if she was suddenly a leper and everyone was afraid of catching her disease. People who'd chatted her up a storm before were suddenly too busy. And it wasn't like she could call the authorities.

But then she'd finally found someone who would talk to her—a guy coming out of Herb Connection carrying a brown paper bag that stank of weed.

"A tall pretty girl? With blondish hair and big—" He'd caught himself before he said *tits*, and instead held his hands to his chest as if he were squeezing melons.

"Yeah," Keely had said, dread settling over her like a shroud. "That's her."

The man told her how he'd seen her get into a limo with Mr. Reaux outside the shop.

"You're sure it was him?"

He'd nodded, said he'd seen the man many times at the dive strip club he owned.

Maybe she should've waited and come up with some sort of plan first, but she couldn't stand the thought of Becca spending one night with that scumbag. Especially when it was Keely's fault that the money hadn't been there on time. When she'd shown up at Aphrodistic asking about Becca, one of the bouncers had ushered her into a dimly lit back room. She'd known she was screwed when she heard the lock engage. Thankfully, he hadn't thought to check the window.

Acutely aware of how high the stakes were, she kissed the stranger with even more intensity. She couldn't let those men from the club, those thugs, get ahold of her, otherwise where would that leave Becca? It wouldn't do either of them any good if they were *both* being held against their will. Plus, this was all her fault. She needed to make this kiss work.

Hitching a knee, she hooked her leg around the man's hip. It shocked the hell out of her when he cupped his hands under her butt and pulled her other leg up, wrapping them both around his waist.

"Thank you," she whispered against his lips.

"You're welcome," he said, his low, rough voice reverberating through her body like a tuning fork.

Her pursuers drew closer. She could feel them looking in this direction. Instinctively, she put up a mental shield, sending invisible jolts of electricity racing down her arms.

The stranger's body shifted slightly.

He hadn't felt that, had he? No, he was reaching for something.

Without breaking the kiss, he turned them so that her back was against the wall. His large frame now stood between her and those men.

Was he protecting her?

Something flashed close to her face.

He had a knife!

Panic and confusion shot through her.

"Shhh. This isn't for you." He ran a thumb over the pulse point on her neck.

His touch was intoxicating and she felt herself relax, although she didn't drop her guard. Almost immediately, he hauled her closer and deepened the kiss, stroking his hand through her hair. He pressed her mouth wider and slipped his tongue inside, acting as if she was his to take. Heat seared through her and desire pooled low in her belly.

Oh God. What was going on? This was all just for show, and yet it felt so...*real*.

Her heart pounded furiously as the two men jogged

past them on the sidewalk, not more than a few feet away. She couldn't tell if her physical reaction was entirely because of them or this darkly compelling man she was kissing.

The moment her pursuers disappeared around the corner, the man took a step backwards and released her. The blade he'd held a moment ago was gone. She disentangled herself, feeling suddenly awkward.

As much as she'd like to duck her head and leave, she knew he deserved some sort of explanation, even if she couldn't tell him the truth.

Now that she was staring up at him from a distance greater than the length of an eyelash, her breath caught in her throat. He stood a good head taller than her, with sleek raven hair pulled into a low bun, warm olive skin and the most intense gray eyes she'd ever seen. He wore a black leather jacket, a plaid shirt underneath, low-slung jeans and black boots with thick soles. If someone were to ask her what two plus two was right now, she'd probably tell them her middle name.

"Um…thanks. I really appreciate…what you did." Sure, he'd just saved her ass, but that was, quite possibly, the most amazing kiss in the history of the world.

"What the hell was that?" he asked, frowning.

It felt as if the balloon she was holding onto had just been popped. He was pissed. She searched his starkly handsome face. Yeah, definitely angry. It wouldn't be the first time she'd ticked off someone with her impulsiveness. Besides, what kind of chick goes around kissing strange men without so much as a hello, anyway?

She opened her mouth to explain herself, but then it hit her. It didn't matter what this man thought of her. He could be pissed. Think of her as a slut. Or a freak. A slutty freak. *Whatever.* Her sister had been kidnapped and she had no idea what she was going to do. Going to the club was the only thing she could think of, and still it wasn't enough. In fact, it had almost turned the situation into an even bigger disaster.

When she didn't answer right away, the man led her into a nearby alley, then turned her to face him, his hands cupping her elbows. "Tell me what just happened. And I want the truth."

"Would you believe me if I said I was overcome by how hot you were and I just couldn't help myself?"

"Then would you believe me if I told you I lived in the penthouse at the top of the Space Needle?" he asked, narrowing his eyes.

She thought it was a rhetorical question, but he was waiting for her answer.

"Uh…no."

He leaned in close. "Don't pull that crap on me, Kitten."

She flinched at his harsh tone, drew her arms close to her body and balled her hands into fists.

He took a step back, a flash of remorse on his face.

"Why were you running?" When she didn't answer right away, he reached forward and twisted a strand of her hair around his finger. "Tell me," he urged softly.

Her bare arms were cold where he'd been touching her. She almost wished he was pissed off again because at least she knew how to deal with that, but concern? From a total stranger? It pierced through her defenses like anger never could, and she felt the sudden, idiotic urge to cry.

Which would be stupid. Very stupid.

She absently twisted the rings on her hands. "I'm fine. Thanks for your help. Those men were after me, that's all."

"Yes, but why?"

She shrugged, not wanting to explain any further if she didn't have to. Even though they were in the Circus District, she didn't dare say anything that would tip him off that she was a Talent. She wasn't feeling up to seeing the revulsion in his eyes. She'd experienced enough of that today.

"Did you steal something?"

Her head snapped up. "For Pete's sake, no! I'm not a thief."

A smile teased the corners of his lips. "Okay, I didn't think so, Kitten."

"Good," she said angrily. "And don't call me that. It's annoying."

"Then what should I call you? Red?"

"Ugh. That's worse."

She considered giving him a fake name, like she and her sister often did when guys would hit on them in a club.

"Tonight, I'm going to be your cousin Mandy visiting from Portland."

"Okay, and I'll be Janna. Our wealthy grandfather just died and left us millions, including his private jet."

"No, then they'll want us to pick up the tab."

"Oh, good point. How about you came up here because Gramps died, and they're going to be reading the will tomorrow? We don't know yet whether we'll be wealthy or not."

"Perfect. It's interesting, gives us lots to talk about, but it's not too far-fetched."

The truth was, she and Becca had more fun creating the pretend backstories than actually using them. More often than not, they just used the names.

Her heart grew heavy at the thought of her sister. And for some reason, she didn't want to lie to this man. At least not about something as trivial as her name.

"I'm Keely."

He cocked his head slightly and nodded thoughtfully.

Wait. He didn't recognize the name, did he? Recognize that she was Bernard Weber's daughter? Was he nodding because it confirmed his suspicions? First there was Cole on the street corner who had recognized her, and now...this.

"Keely," he repeated, as if trying out her name on his lips. Her heart sped up just a touch. "I'm Toryn." His smile was genuine, but hesitant, as if he didn't do it much.

Her paranoia disappeared. He didn't know who she was.

But now she felt awkward again. Had she really just made out with this man? Because, seriously. He was So. Freaking. Hot.

A cool breeze from the bay blew through the alley, making her suddenly aware that she was no longer wearing her sweatshirt. Adrenaline and nerves had made her forget. "Thanks for…um…everything." The air had also blown some sense into her. It was time to go. Get back to the shop. Figure out what to do about Becca. She flipped her hand up, giving a little wave. "I'll…uh…catch you later."

He stepped in front of her, blocking her exit. Then he took off his leather jacket and held it out. "I'll walk you to your car."

"Thanks, but I'm good," she said, declining both the jacket and the offer. "I walked and I don't live far."

"Well," he said, draping his jacket over her shoulders anyway. "You are not walking home alone."

She really should continue to protest. But the coat was so warm. And, if she were being honest with herself, she liked how the man's protectiveness made her feel. Safe. Less alone.

She hadn't realized just how chilled to the bone she was until now. Pulling the lapel tightly around her neck, she took a deep breath of the leather.

Mmmm. It smelled like him.

She thought about what she would she say to him when they got to her shop. How would she explain it? One look and he would know she was a Talent. That he'd kissed a freak.

And she wasn't sure she could handle that right now. Not from this man.

———————

A range of emotions tore through Toryn as he looked down at the petite, curvy woman who'd been in his arms a moment ago. Thick strands of red hair spilled over her shoulders, now covered by his leather coat. Various piercings studded her ears, and she had a smaller stud in her right nostril. Her cheeks were flushed, lips red—not from lipstick but from that…kiss.

Holy Fates. Could that kiss have been any hotter? If she weren't in front of him right now, he might have thought he'd dreamt the whole thing.

Hazel eyes flecked with green and gold stared up at him unblinking, as if daring him to challenge her. Like she was expecting blowback from him and was ready to take him on.

Even while being chased by two thugs, this woman

had been able to think on her feet, concoct a plan in an instant, and execute it perfectly. He respected the hell out of anyone who could do that.

When he wrapped his coat around her, he'd caught a glimpse of a butterfly tattoo peeking out from under the strap of her tank top. He'd wanted to run a finger underneath the strap and push it aside to see the whole design.

The woman was beautiful. Stunningly so. With an edge to her that said you either accepted her for who she was or you got out of her way. He was drawn to her strength, found it incredibly attractive.

And distracting as hell.

He had work to do. Needed to get back to the stakeout. He'd been gone long enough, and the other warriors were probably wondering where the hell he was. He needed to tell them about the Town Cars. Reaux might be at the club now.

With the back of his hand, he rubbed off the taste of her kiss from his mouth. It had been too long since he'd been with a woman if a simple kiss could get to him like this.

She glanced around nervously, probably looking for her pursuers.

"They're long gone. You gave them the slip."

"I hope so." She flashed him a tight smile. "I...I think I can get it from here."

"This isn't exactly a safe neighborhood this time of

night." He'd witnessed a few drug deals go down and had run into a number of questionable characters, including a sonofabitch who tried to mug a homeless man. Toryn had seen to it that the bloke wouldn't think about doing that again for a real long time. "Where do you live?"

She pointed down the alley. "It's not far."

It occurred to him that she didn't want him to know where she lived, but he could no more let her walk home alone than he could stand idly by and watch an old man get mugged. "Then I'll see you to your door."

Without waiting for her to reply, he ushered her down the alley, where they stepped around a drunk passed out next to the Dumpster. A dark, rat-sized shape ran along the edge of the building just ahead of them.

"So are you going to tell me what you did back there or not?

His jacket was so big on her that he nearly missed her shrug. "It was called a kiss," she retorted.

He chuckled. Should've seen that coming. Why so evasive, though? He wondered how far he could push her. "I'm talking about that jolt of electricity, Kitten. What was that?"

Something flared in her expression then quickly disappeared. If he'd been further away and not studying her intently, he'd have missed it.

Surprise? Yes, that was what it was. And worry.

"I have no idea what you're talking about."

His eyes narrowed. She was lying, and he had a pretty good idea why.

That was a Talent's energy he'd felt, and she clearly didn't want him to know about it.

But before he could ask any other questions, a sound behind them drew his attention. He turned to see a Night Patrol vehicle moving slowly past the mouth of the alley. Then it stopped.

Almost instantly, the two of them flattened themselves against the brick building, the Dumpster to their left and several old plastic chairs to their right.

A run-in with the authorities was the last thing he needed. His papers weren't exactly legit.

In the darkness, he could just make out her expression. It was one of sheer panic as she chewed on the inside of her cheek. He had the sudden urge to pull her into his arms, reassure her that everything was going to be okay.

A beam of light cut through the night. If they'd been on the other side of the Dumpster, they would have been in plain sight, but as it was, they were hidden.

"Hey, you down there. What's going on?"

Before Toryn could figure out what to do or say, a voice—a man's voice—called out. "Trying to get a little shut eye." It was the drunk they'd stepped over a moment ago.

"Who's with you?"

The man lifted his head, looked straight at Toryn and

smiled. Then he turned back to the police. "No one. I'm here alone. Now will you please shut that off and let me be? I'm tired."

The light clicked off and the alley was awash in inky black again.

Toryn glanced over to gauge Keely's reaction. His leather coat was draped over one of the chairs next to him, and she was gone.

CHAPTER THREE

$\mathcal{A}$ string of obscenities rang through the Iron Haven, its unfinished rooms acting as amplifiers for the noise. Toryn had been out in the garage, working on a custom piece of furniture that would go in the library, when he heard the commotion and came running.

When he arrived in the kitchen, Asher was standing in the middle of the room, hopping from foot to foot, cradling his hand like a baby. There was a hammer lying in the middle of the floor.

"Son of a bitch!"

Toryn half expected to see blood spurting, but there were only a few drops on the sawdust-covered subfloor at the other man's feet.

Rickert, the leader of the Iron Guild warriors, had just arrived. He looked mildly irritated. It had better not be a waste of his time that he'd dropped what he was doing. The guy did *not* like getting interrupted. Vince and Zara were across the room, out of breath as if they'd just sprinted the entire length of the house.

Olivia had her hand on Asher's back. "Let me see it."

"It's nothing—I'm fine. Everyone, just leave me alone. Go back to what you were doing."

"I expected to see a bloody stump given all that racket," Rickert said wryly.

"Come on." Olivia tugged at his arm.

"No healing, okay?"

She was a Healer-Talent, able to mend tissue and bone, but Asher didn't like his fiancé to use her special abilities very often, and certainly not on him, because it took so much out of her.

"I just want to take a look."

He reluctantly relinquished his hand, and she gently opened up his fingers. "Jeez, Ash, you really did a number on the end of your thumb. It's crushed. This does not look like nothing."

Then Sean came into the kitchen. Unlike everyone else who'd been working on the renovation of the old mansion, he'd been sitting around on his ass, staring at a computer screen. If he wanted to be treated as a team player, he sure as hell wasn't acting like one.

"Want me to take a look at it?" he asked.

Toryn tried not to laugh. The only medical training

the guy had was as the self-appointed medic in his prison.

Asher's head snapped up. "I do not want to be pricked or prodded, Sean. Sorry."

Several people laughed.

Sean finally succeeded in getting Asher to let him see his hand. He manipulated the various joints as Asher gritted his teeth.

"Yep. It'll need to be stitched and splinted. The tip is definitely broken. And you should probably get a tetanus shot."

"No." Asher yanked his hand away.

Olivia crossed her arms. "You're going to have to let me heal it then." When he started to protest, she held out her hands for him to stop. "Your choice, babe. It's a quick fix. It'll barely make a dent in me. Healing you rarely does. But if it will make you feel better, I'll go upstairs and lie down afterwards. Or Sean can do it his way, but—no offense—my way is faster and much less painful."

"None taken," Sean said.

"All I need is some ointment and butterfly bandages," Asher muttered, "and I'll be fine."

Olivia let out an exasperated sigh. "Listen. You might as well know that I'll just heal you when you're sleeping tonight. No use fighting me about it. I can do it now and be done with it, or you can be stubborn and spend the rest of the day in agony until I fix it after you fall asleep."

Asher scowled. "What happened to those days when you *had* to do what I told you?"

"Those days are loooong gone," she said, snapping her fingers. "Now give me your hand."

"Holy Fates, how I miss those days," he muttered.

Zara snickered from across the room at her brother.

Asher glared at his sister. "What are you laughing at?"

Olivia looked over at Zara. "Has he always been like this?"

Zara nodded. "A baby? Difficult? Bossy? Unfortunately, all of the above."

"Glad I have so much support around here from the people I love." Asher made a low, guttural sound then begrudgingly held out his hand to Olivia. "Okay, do it."

She gave him a quick kiss on the mouth. "I'll be fine. Promise."

Placing her hands on the bare skin of his forearm, she closed her eyes and concentrated. It took only a few moments for the skin to knit back together and the bone underneath to mend.

Sean was transfixed as Olivia worked her magic. "Simply amazing."

"You've never run across a Healer-Talent before, Sean?" Rickert asked curiously.

The man shook his head. "Back in college, there was a woman in the class ahead of me who left school abruptly. Rumor had it that she was a healer. But I never saw what she could do."

"What happened to her?" Zara asked. There was a slight catch in her voice.

Sean shook his head. "Don't know."

"I'll tell ye what happened," Rickert said, scuffing up the sawdust under his boots. "She was forced to give up everything and join the bloody army."

The man's anger was well founded. Something similar had happened to his fiancée, who had once owned a thriving costume design business. Clearly it still rankled, even though it had happened before they met. Neyla was expecting their first baby and designing clothes again. Although Toryn seriously didn't get the whole fashion thing, she apparently was making a name for herself already. Recently, he and a few of the other warriors had been in one of the open-air markets when he'd overheard a group of women raving about Neyla's shop, saying they were on her waiting list.

Zara coughed. "Or resist and spend years in prison while the army tries to break you."

Vince pulled her into his arms and pressed a soothing kiss to the top of her head. "We know all about that, don't we, Sean?"

The big man rubbed a hand over his close-cropped black hair and nodded.

Asher was flexing the fingers and thumb of his injured hand over and over.

"How does it feel?" Olivia asked, a faint shadow of fatigue hovering under her eyes now.

"Perfect, Lass. As good as new. Thank you." Then he brushed his lips tenderly over hers and led her out of the kitchen, presumably up to their room to tuck her into bed.

Everyone turned then and went back to what they were doing. Sean looked stunned, as if he still couldn't quite believe what he'd just witnessed. He went back to the table and took up his position in front of the computer screen again.

Toryn picked up Asher's hammer from the middle of the floor and set it on the counter.

The renovations on this Iron Haven—the second one —wouldn't be finished anytime soon. There were whole wings that hadn't even been touched yet.

It had been Rickert and Neyla's idea to set up a few places for warriors to call home while on this side of the portal, since you couldn't cross back over for a few weeks without getting iron sick. The compound had once been a resort for the rich and famous at the beginning of the last century until a flood wiped out the only road leading in. It lay abandoned for decades, forgotten by Pacificans. But just to be on the safe side, Esmerelda crystals had been brought over and strategically placed around the property's perimeter, hiding it from the outside world.

Toryn turned to head back out to the garage when something on Sean's screen caught his attention.

"What's that?" he asked, stepping closer to get a better look.

Sean glanced up, surprise registering on his face before he looked back at his screen. "Pictures I took of the club the other night. I thought maybe I could figure out another way in. See that window up on the second floor?" He enlarged the image. "It looks like it's open. I was thinking we could..."

Sean kept talking but Toryn wasn't listening. He was looking at something else in the image.

"Those men. Down at the bottom. Who are they?"

"The bouncers, I think. Hold on." Sean pressed a few buttons. Toryn wasn't very familiar with computers or how digital cameras worked, but whatever the man did, that section of the picture got bigger.

"Yeah, those are the bouncers, and that one there," Sean said, touching the screen, "is the Psychic-Talent who ousted Asher and Konal."

"What the bloody hell?" Toryn rubbed a hand over the stubble on his chin, confused as hell. They were the same two men who had chased Keely. "Are you sure?"

"Yes."

"Did the Psychic-Talent shake their hands?" he asked. "Make skin to skin contact? Is that how he read their minds and knew what they were there for?"

Sean shook his head. "I don't think so. As soon as

they got about ten feet from the entrance, the bouncers just knew."

No skin-to-skin contact. The Psychics he knew had to be touching you to read your mind. But if that thug's Talent was so powerful, why hadn't he read their thoughts when Toryn and Keely were kissing? The men had paused on the sidewalk less than ten feet away then sprinted off. If the Talent had been able to read their minds, he would've known that Keely was the one they were chasing and that the man she was kissing was plotting to kill their boss.

Since Konal or Asher could easily corroborate Sean's claim that this was the same guy, Toryn had to assume he was telling the truth.

Then he remembered the jolt of electricity when Keely had kissed him. And it couldn't be chalked up to his reaction to having that hot young woman throw herself into his arms and press that sweet little body of hers to his. He slowly rubbed his palms together at the memory of how luscious her curves were, and he ached to have her in his arms again.

No, as electrifying as that kiss was, what he'd felt was something different.

Keely had done something. Something to block their thoughts from her pursuers.

He'd suspected she was a Talent, but could she be a Shield-Talent, someone who was immune from the psychic attacks from other Talents? And if so, could she have shielded him as well? Holy Fates. Was that even possible?

Toryn grabbed two beers from the kitchen and handed one to Sean who mumbled a quick thanks.

If his hunch was correct, maybe he could use Keely's Talent to get into the nightclub. With her by his side, he could waltz in and kill Reaux right under their noses. Those bodyguards would have no clue what was going to happen until it was too late.

Plus, it would give him the perfect excuse to see her again.

It was absurd that he couldn't stop thinking about her, couldn't get her off his mind. He tried to brush it off as no big deal—hell, he'd kissed plenty of women before this one—but there was something so…different about her. He took a long swig of his beer, trying to recall if he'd ever been this intrigued by a woman before. But then, he'd never had a woman throw herself at him like that before either. She'd roused all of his male instincts.

But he couldn't let himself get too carried away. He'd once made that mistake with a Cascadian girl he thought he had feelings for. Turned out she was only using him to get through a portal into Pacifica and left him the first chance she got. He would not make that same mistake by trusting the wrong person again.

Other than the fact that Keely lived somewhere in or around the Circus District, he didn't know much about her. He didn't even know her last name. How would he be able to find her? She'd taken off without a word. One minute they were together in the alley and the next minute she was gone. She'd been reluctant to tell him much, but just when it seemed as if she was going to open up to him, the Night Patrol had shown up and spooked her. That girl had secrets and he wanted to know what they were.

He looked at Sean. The man was built like a tank—probably pushing six-six or six-seven—with cords of muscle on top of muscle, his dark skin straining to keep it all in. He looked like a professional body builder, someone whose physical prowess was his most important asset. Not like a guy who spent hours and hours studying and writing computer code before the army got hold of him.

"Vince tells me you're a Tracker-Talent," Toryn said.

Sean nodded but kept pecking away on the keyboard.

"What do ye need in order to…uh, track someone?"

Sean was probably wondering why the warrior who hated him the most was asking him all these questions. "An article of the target's clothing is best," he said, his tone even.

Damn. He didn't have anything that belonged to Keely.

Pushing away a strand of hair that had slipped into his face, Toryn quickly redid the knot at his nape and thought about the trashcan where she'd stuffed her sweatshirt. It was probably long gone by now. Then he saw his leather jacket hanging over the back of a nearby chair.

"What about something the...the target recently wore?" He felt a twinge of guilt about referring to Keely in such a callous manner, like she wasn't really a person but a means to an end. He couldn't forget the look of sheer terror in her eyes.

Sean frowned and thought for a moment. "But he or she doesn't own it?"

"No. Is ownership of an item important?"

"That's part of it, yes." His dark eyes scanned Toryn's face.

He was probably thinking: *Why should I help this asshole? He's been nothing but a jerk to me.*

But then he said, "I'm certainly willing to give it a try."

CHAPTER FOUR

Keely carried the cup of water through the tattoo parlor and handed it to the customer at Verla's station.

"Thanks," the man said, then knocked it back as if it were a shot of whiskey.

Verla looked up at him over the rims of her glasses. "You doing okay, hon? Want to take a short break?"

"Yeah, that would be great," he said, sounding relieved. "Need to hit the john, make a couple of phone calls."

According to the girl at the front desk, Verla had been working on the guy's intricate sleeve pattern for over an hour.

"Right on," Verla said, setting down the needle and stripping off her black latex gloves. "Meet you back here in ten?"

"Sure." The man pushed himself up from the chair with grunt and headed toward the bathrooms.

For the past two days, Keely had sent countless texts to Becca, but all of them had gone unanswered. Up until now, she'd spent every waking moment in the bookstore, sitting near the front door. She only left her post if she had a customer. Whenever a car turned down the street, she jumped, straining to see if it was Mr. Reaux's limo bringing Becca home.

"It was all a terrible misunderstanding," he would say. *"I did not mean to worry you. Please, accept my apologies..."*

But of course that never happened. Becca was still gone, and Keely had no idea what to do to get her back. She hoped her sister was still in the Circus District somewhere. No doubt she was scared. Terrified, even. Had that bastard hurt her? Was she calling out for help but there was no one to hear her?

Keely pressed a hand to her forehead to quell the rising panic. When they were kids, they used to pretend they could communicate with their thoughts, giving each other hard stares from across the room in an attempt to transmit what they were thinking. If only that was her Talent. She'd know where her sister was and could come in with guns blazing and rescue her. If she had a gun. Okay, maybe a knife then. She could get a knife, a thin little switchblade that would fit in her pocket, then go there and stab that sonofabitch.

She sighed. Being a Shield-Talent—a crappy one

whose abilities to ward off other Talents were limited and sporadic—would not cut it. She was only kick-ass and tough in her imagination.

Becca, on the other hand, was good at what she did. With a simple touch, she was able to project various thoughts and feelings to another person, get them to believe all sorts of outlandish things—a Talent that came in handy when selling *fortunes*. If Becca had been able to use it to get away from her captors, she would have done it already. Or prevented herself from being taken in the first place. The thing was, Mr. Reaux knew the people he extorted money from were Talents. He probably knew how to prevent—

Hell, maybe *he* was a Shield-Talent and immune to anything Becca could dish out. Just like Keely.

If only she and Becca weren't Talents. Then she'd call the authorities and let them handle this. But that wasn't the case, and she was Becca's only hope. The buck stopped at her.

For a fleeting moment in the alley, she'd almost confided in Toryn when he demanded to know what was going on. He was so insistent that she nearly caved. But no matter how safe she felt in his presence, she couldn't risk telling him the truth. There was too much at stake.

Panic and worry clawed up her spine again at what Becca must be going through. She didn't want to think about it. She just wanted her sister back.

After Verla covered her workstation, Keely followed her out the back service door, where her friend lit up a cigarette. Harvey, the owner of Freak Ink, was out having a smoke, too. (It sounded like *free kink* when you said it fast, which was how Harvey wanted it pronounced when someone answered the phone.)

"I know you're worried, Keely," Verla said. "I'm sure it's just one of Reaux's scare tactics. You'll see."

"What's going on?" Harvey asked, frowning.

Keely explained to him what had happened as she absently picked at the label on the bottle of water she'd grabbed on the way out. The lump in her throat that she'd been trying to ignore gave way to a sob. "It's…it's my fault she's gone."

Harvey cursed under his breath.

Exhaling a puff of smoke, Verla stepped over and put a hand on Keely's shoulder. "Like it was your fault you got mugged on your way home from the bank by an angry mob of self-righteous protesters? *Bastards.*"

Harvey spat out a short burst of brown spit then took another drag of his cigarette. Guess if you wanted a nicotine hit, you might as well go all in. She wouldn't be surprised if he were chewing a piece of nicotine gum, too.

"There's something going on over at Aphrodistic," he said. "Something very hush-hush."

Keely's breath hitched. "What kind of something? Why do you think it could involve Becca?"

He shrugged. "I don't know for sure. One of my regulars is a bartender there. But given that a few other Talents have gone missing after talking to Reaux—attractive young women like your sister—I'm just guessing it's related."

"There have been others?" she asked, her eyes widening. "Who?"

"You know that girl who works at the coffee place?"

There were dozens of coffee shops and carts in the District, but she had a pretty good idea who he meant. "You mean Hanna from Circus Coffee?"

Hanna, a former dancer who quit to have her son, was a popular bikini barista. Word would get out on social media that she was working the coffee cart that day, and within minutes there'd be a long line. Suddenly every male in the area, and some females, needed a caffeine fix. An old man on a video ad for Circus Coffee proclaimed he goes there to get a drink from Hanna because it's the biggest thrill of his day.

"That's the one," Harvey said. "I was talking to Yvonne—"

"The woman who owns the cart?" Verla interrupted.

"Yeah, Yvonne. That's her. I ran into her this morning when I was out walking Fritz. Turns out Hanna missed her shift yesterday. A few customers saw her talking the night before to Davin Reaux."

"Okay, so Hanna's missing, too," Keely said

impatiently. "But can we focus on what your bartender friend told you?"

"Apparently they're getting ready for some big private event over there. The whole place will be shutting down to get ready for it."

Verla examined her cuticles. "They gonna bleach it out from top to bottom?"

"Private event?" Keely asked. She didn't like the sound of that. "What kind of private event?"

Harvey shrugged. "My friend doesn't know many details. Just that a bunch of VIPs will be in attendance."

"What kind of a VIP," Verla said with air quotes, "goes to an event at Aphrodistic?"

Harvey flicked an ash from his cigarette. "Apparently some heavy hitters. My client thought there were going to be a few professional athletes, politicians. Maybe a rock star or two. All the staff has to sign NDAs. And they've let a bunch of people go."

Keely chewed on her lip. But what did this all have to do with Becca? She'd heard about establishments that catered to the rich and famous, only hiring beautiful people to work there. Women who had a certain look… and certain measurements.

The door to the alley opened and the receptionist poked her head out. "Steve is waiting for you, Verla. Are you—?"

"Oh, shit, yeah," she said, stubbing out her cigarette. "Tell him I'm coming."

Harvey held the door open for them.

Keely started to follow Verla back inside when her phone rang.

"I'll be right in," she told them.

She pulled the phone from her pocket, glanced at the screen, and her heart nearly stopped.

It was Becca.

By the time Toryn and Sean arrived back in New Seattle, the sun had already dipped below the Olympic Mountains to the west, leaving in its wake a thin, gray light. Rush hour was nearly over, most of the commuters having left for home on earlier trains and ferries. For the most part, the sidewalks were scattered with well-dressed and well-behaved people heading to dinners and cocktail hours. It was still too early for the rowdier nightlife crowd.

An array of tantalizing aromas greeted them when they got to the Circus District. Indian curry. Italian pasta. Vietnamese pho. New Seattle seafood. Neither Toryn nor Sean had eaten anything since they left the Iron Haven, so they might have to grab something from one of the street vendors soon.

Sean stood on the corner and looked up and down the street several times. In one hand was Toryn's leather coat, the one that Keely had worn for a short time. She'd looked so charming, so enticing, with his large jacket draped over her curvy, petite frame, he thought, and a sudden wave of possessiveness surged through him.

"Don't you have to smell it or something?" Toryn asked, confused.

Sean shook his head. "It's more of an energy marker that I'm trying to match up, not exactly a scent, although that's the easiest way to think of it."

"So are you getting anything yet?" He was unable to keep the impatience out of his tone. Sean had told him it would be a long shot, but that didn't keep him from hoping for success.

"No."

They started at the edge of the District, walking the area in a grid pattern so as not to miss a single side street or alley. There were no skyscrapers in this part of town, just a bunch of historic five- and six-story buildings that had clearly seen better days. Sean told him that it had once been a trendy part of town back before the big earthquake hit and turned much of it to rubble.

They had just passed a boarded-up building with a bright orange condemned sign tacked to the front when Sean stopped.

"What?" Toryn asked, almost bumping into him. "Do you have something?"

"I can't tell," the other man said, frowning. "But I'm

picking up something familiar. It's coming from somewhere over there."

Toryn turned his attention in that direction. There was a nondescript building across the street and next to it, a small patch of open space that the city called a park but which was actually only a few benches and a square of grass.

He scanned the people, looking for that telltale mane of red hair. Nothing.

Several food trucks were parked on the curb, but he didn't see her in any of the lines either. Sean was saying something about being hungry, but Toryn wasn't listening.

Maybe Keely was inside one of the stores. There was a vegan donut shop that offered palm readings, a pawnshop that promised top dollar for the wedding ring your bastard ex-husband gave you, and Mental Travel, an agency that promised you the vacation of your dreams.

When he saw the tattoo parlor at the far end, he remembered the butterfly tattoo on Keely's shoulder. Was that where she'd gotten it? Maybe she was there now. A surge of excitement shot through him at the thought of coming face-to-face with her again. But if not, maybe the people inside would know her and could put him in touch with her.

"Listen, I think I may know where she could be," he

told Sean. "If you want to go grab something to eat, I can meet up with you later."

Although he was starting to trust the guy a little more, he didn't want him hanging around if he did run into Keely. Not if he could help it. There'd be introductions, explanations. It would be easier if he were alone.

Disappointment flashed in Sean's eyes for a moment before disappearing. "Why don't you take this then?" He handed Toryn a cell phone.

Toryn stared at the device but didn't take it. Iron Guild warriors didn't use cell phones. Before the Iron Havens were built, warriors had nowhere to keep material possessions on this side of the portal. But more importantly, the Pacifican army was known to monitor and eavesdrop on cell phone conversations, and they couldn't take that risk. Not when the location of portals and the lives of Cascadians were at stake.

"I jail-broke it," Sean explained. "Then rerouted the network to a hidden frequency and removed all location identifiers."

"Care to explain that in English?" Toryn asked gruffly.

"It means that no one else will be able to listen in on your conversations. Just the person on the other end of the line. And no one will be able to ping the phone to figure out its location. Rickert is having me procure them for all the warriors to use when they're on this side of the portal."

Toryn still wasn't sure what all that meant, but if Rickert was okay with it, then that was good enough for him. He took the phone from Sean, and the guy gave him a crash course on how it worked.

"I'll grab a bite to eat and then if I don't hear from you, I will…uh…run a couple of errands. So no hurry. Just call me if you need me for any reason."

"Thanks. I appreciate that."

Toryn thought he detected a hint of sadness in the guy's demeanor. He debated whether to say anything or not. Finally, his curiosity got the best of him. "Everything okay?"

Sean met his gaze for a moment then looked away. "Yeah, I'm fine."

"Are you sure? Because if there's something I can do…" He let the offer trail off.

The truth was, he owed him. The guy had done him a solid today, even though Toryn had been a total dick ever since they met. Rickert had him working on computer stuff back at the Iron Haven. There was plenty for him to do, and yet he'd dropped everything in order to help Toryn.

Sean rubbed a hand over his face. "It's nothing really. I just thought I'd swing by my old neighborhood. See if I can get a glimpse of my family from the street."

Ah. So that explained why the guy had been so

willing to help. "You still don't think it's safe to let them know you're okay?"

Sean shook his head. "It will never be safe. I cannot take that chance. It's not worth it." He cleared the emotion from his throat then looked up to the sky, as if searching the heavens for strength. "I'd rather my wife move on and my daughter grow up without me than have them be in danger again because of me."

Guilt for being so distrustful of this man stabbed at Toryn like a blunt knife.

This was a dangerous line of work they were in, fighting against the Pacifican army. With the exception of Rickert, Asher and Vince—whose women were as tough as they were—all the warriors with families kept them on the other side of the portal. And for good reason. They'd be prime targets for the army if they knew about them.

But Sean wasn't a warrior. After heavy lobbying from a few of the men, he was released from the jail pits, but he was banished from Cascadia forever. He was a man without a home.

Sean nodded once, pressed his lips into a thin line. "Good luck. I hope you find her."

Toryn wanted to say that he hoped Sean was successful, too, that he'd somehow be able to get a glimpse of his loved ones when he drove through his old neighborhood. But he kept his mouth shut. Even for him, that would be too cruel.

CHAPTER FIVE

Something wasn't right.

Pressing the phone to her ear and covering the other one with her free hand, Keely strained to hear what her sister was saying.

Becca didn't sound like herself. Something was off about her. Like she was under the influence of someone…or something.

Crap. Was she using again?

Becca used to have a drug problem, back when they were going through all that stuff with their parents, but that was behind her now. She'd been clean for years.

Becca should've been yelling at Keely that she hadn't gotten to the shop with the money on time. Or pleading with her to help, to do something to get her away from her captors.

But Becca was saying none of those things. In fact,

she didn't even sound frightened. Rather, she was going on and on about some great opportunity. Kept referring to it as her "big break."

Keely didn't understand. Was her sister being coerced or threatened into saying this? "Becca, what's going on? Can you tell me the truth?"

"Aren't you listening?" Becca said impatiently. "I'm trying to tell you."

"So…a guy kidnaps you and you're okay with that?"

Just then, the door to Freak Ink opened and another one of Harvey's people came out for a smoke. Keely hurried around the corner for some privacy and took a seat on one of the park benches.

"He did not kidnap me, Keely."

"Then what do you call it?"

"He came to the shop, and sure, he wanted to know about the money. But we talked. And I left with him. It's as simple as that."

"Yeah, without so much as a note. That's not like you. Tell me what's really going on. Is someone there with you right now? Is that why you're talking like this, because this doesn't make sense?"

Becca sighed. "Everything's fine, Keely. I wish you would stop overreacting."

Overreacting? This was not *fine*. She decided just to come right out with it. "Are you using again? Is that what this is about?"

Becca laughed. "You think I'm on a bender?"

"Well, are you?"

"I don't have to listen to your BS, Keely."

Anger surged through her. The Becca she knew—the clean and sober Becca—would never do something like this. "Well, what am I supposed to think? The man comes to the shop to collect his hush money and then you leave with him, voluntarily, without even telling me? No call. No note. No nothing. Do you have any idea how worried I've been?"

"Sorry, Kee." There was a muffled sound on the other end of the line. When she spoke again, her tone was different. "You sound jealous of me."

Keely choked. "Jealous?"

"Yeah, because *I'm* going to be having the time of my life and *you* weren't invited."

Being kidnapped and being invited were two totally different things, but she was done arguing with Becca. You didn't try to reason with an addict who was clearly using again. "Where are you anyway? Who's with you? Is *he* there?"

Becca laughed. "I'm fine. Really." She sounded mellow. Too mellow. "I'll be home tomorrow afternoon. We'll talk more then. You'll see...everything is going to be great."

Relief rushed through her that Becca would be coming home. "Thank God." Maybe she could talk some sense into her then.

"Yeah, I'll be by to pick up my things."

The relief she felt came crashing to a halt. "You'll be leaving again?"

"You can handle the shop for a few weeks by yourself, can't you?"

"I...uh..."

"Listen, we'll talk more tomorrow. Okay?"

There was another muffled sound on the other end of the line and then a click.

"Becca? Becca?"

The line was dead.

Keely's hands shook as she stared down at her phone. She considered calling their mother, then decided against it. They hadn't talked in almost three years. Not since that horrible Christmas when she and Becca had tried to patch things up with them. Besides, what could her mother do? Not only did she have a hard time getting around after being injured in a train station bombing, she was LUI. Living under the influence...of a jerk.

"Hey. Are you okay?" It was a man's voice. A very familiar, deep male voice.

Keely's breath caught in her throat as a large pair of boots came into view in front of her. Slowly, she lifted her gaze.

Black combat fatigues. Long legs set shoulder-width apart. Powerful thighs. Slim hips. Charcoal T-shirt stretched over flat abs and a muscular chest. Leather coat, unzipped. Broad shoulders. A ruggedly handsome face with striking gray eyes staring down at her.

"Toryn?"

Before she could wonder how he'd found her or what he was doing here, he took a seat next to her on the bench. He reached out as if to take her hand then changed his mind and folded his arms across his chest instead.

His gaze raked over her, his pupils two dark specks of intensity. "What happened? Did someone hurt you?" His nostrils flared slightly and a muscle in his jaw ticked. It looked as if he were capable of ripping off someone's head right now.

She found his outrage on her behalf strangely comforting and shook her head. "No, no. I'm fine. It's… it's my sister."

"What about your sister?" he demanded.

She took a deep breath and wondered where to start. "She's in trouble. Bad trouble. It's all my fault and I don't know what to do." She covered her face with her hands.

She felt Toryn's hand on her back. His touch was calm and soothing amidst the chaos spinning out of control in her head.

And just like that, she spilled everything. Toryn sat there and listened patiently. Not once did she get the vibe that he was repulsed that she and her sister were Talents. It was a relief, almost cathartic, to talk to him about what had happened.

"So the other night when I ran into you," she said, "I'd gone to Mr. Reaux's club to find Becca. To reason with him. You know, come up with some sort of payment plan and—"

"Reaux? As in *Davin* Reaux?" Anger flashed in Toryn's dark eyes. "That's who came for your sister?"

"You know him?"

Toryn cursed, scrubbed a hand over his face as if he were trying to wipe away what he'd just heard. "You went to confront Reaux? What the bloody hell were you thinking?"

What was I thinking? Wasn't it obvious?

"He has my sister! What else was I supposed to do?"

"That was foolish, Keely. And stupid."

She jumped to her feet and started to leave. She didn't need his criticism. She'd been criticized enough in her life, thank you very much. Clearly, she'd made an error in judgment opening up to this man.

He stood, grabbed her wrist and pulled her back. She hit his chest with an *oomph*. She tried to take a step backwards, but he wouldn't let go.

"Reaux is a sadistic, dangerous son of a bitch, Keely. Ye shouldn't have tried to handle this situation on your own."

She was vaguely aware that he'd lapsed into a foreign accent.

"What? And call the authorities? Admitting my sister and I are Talents would get me a one-way ticket to army boot camp." She punched his chest in frustration. "So I'm supposed to wait around for something to happen? Hope the guy changes his mind? Well, I'm not a piece of driftwood, hoping that someday the tide will take pity on me and take me where I want to go. I make things happen or I go down fighting."

Something flickered in his eyes, but she was too angry to care what it was.

"Confronting him isn't the answer." His tone was a little softer. With a hand on her back, he held her closer, and this time she didn't fight him.

"Easy for you to say," she said, suddenly aware of how muscular he was. "In a perfect world, I'd have some recourse. But then, in a perfect world, my sister and I wouldn't have to pay over a week's worth of profits to that jerk just to keep the army from raiding our business and dragging us away."

Toryn remained quiet for a few minutes, a rock of strength before her. She felt the rise and fall of his chest as she breathed in his brisk, masculine scent, and her anger started to melt. It felt nice like this. In his arms. A respite in the face of a rising storm.

She relaxed a fraction. "Becca says she'll be back tomorrow afternoon, so hopefully I'll find out what's going on."

"Very well then," he said, as if he'd just made up his mind. "Come on."

She cranked her head up to look at him. "Where are we going?"

"To get you something to eat and then I'm taking you home."

Toryn left the food truck carrying two plates of food and set them on the picnic table where Keely was sitting.

"Thanks." She handed him a napkin and a small package of plastic utensils, then wasted no time spearing a piece of meat from her plate and popping it into her mouth. She quickly followed that up with a huge bite of noodles.

He enjoyed watching her eat and smiled to himself as he unwrapped his fork. Women here didn't normally eat with such enthusiasm. Seeing her take pleasure in something as simple as a plate of food made him wonder what else made her happy.

She must've noticed his amusement, because she looked embarrassed and covered her mouth with a hand. "Sorry, I'm really hungry, I guess. Can't remember when I last sat down for a meal. Plus, their balsamic-glazed beef with homemade garlic noodles is one of my favorites."

"You've been worried. That's understandable. Makes it hard to eat." A fact he knew too well. He hadn't been able to eat much the summer his father died. It took a long time to get his appetite back at the orphanage. Had his mother taken him in, it still would've been hard, but she wasn't interested. After abandoning him and his father when Toryn was a baby, she wanted nothing to do with him...even after his father's death.

He shoved those thoughts away and turned his attention on his ridiculously tiny fork. He was tempted to use his fingers like they often did back home, but that wasn't done over here. People would see that and instantly peg him as a savage, a barbarian from Cascadia.

Despite the fork challenges, he eventually managed to make it work and he took a big bite. No wonder Keely was shoveling it in. The meat was tender and flavorful. And the noodles *were* delicious.

He thought about their earlier conversation. "I'm not surprised to hear you are a Talent."

She looked around before turning her attention back to him. "Why?"

"I felt the signs of it when you were kissing me," he said, trying hard not to slip into his Cascadian accent.

She lowered her eyes and concentrated on twirling noodles with her fork. "I...I'm really sorry about that. It was rude."

He wasn't sure he understood her. "Rude?"

"You know. Not polite. I shouldn't have used my Talent on you without your permission."

"I don't know what you're talking about, Kitten. It

was not offensive to me." Quite the opposite, in fact. It had been almost as intimate as that kiss.

Her mouth quirked, not quite a smile.

"You're a Shield-Talent, aren't you?" he asked softly.

"Yeah, I guess so, but I've never had much of a handle on it. If you were to ask my father, he'd call me a manipulator."

"Whatever you did, I'm grateful. It prevented a Psychic-Talent thug from reading our minds."

She stopped twisting her noodles and looked up. "Are you talking about those guys chasing me?"

He frowned. Didn't she know? "One of them was a Psychic-Talent. I assumed that's why you put up that mental shield. That you did it on purpose."

She shook her head. "I…I…don't know what I did. I just kept wishing they would run past us…and they did." She gazed at him, a curious look on her face. "Why are *you* grateful they weren't able to read your mind?"

He couldn't exactly tell her that he was a warrior from Cascadia. People here didn't look kindly on those they thought were terrorists. "Let's just say had they known my intentions, they'd have been after me, too." He needed to change the focus of this conversation. "So why did you say it was rude?"

She shrugged. "That's what I was taught. You don't flaunt something that should be kept locked away."

"Locked away like a shameful secret? So your family doesn't consider your Talent a gift?"

Her laugh was bitter. "Hardly. When they found out about my sister and me, they kicked us out of the house. I was fifteen. Becca was seventeen. Given that my mom was permanently disabled by a bombing a few years ago, you'd think they would have called the army to see if they could use our Talents in their fight against the terrorists. Guess I should be thankful they didn't."

He let out a slow exhale and let her words sink in. If she believed Cascadian warriors were responsible for hurting her mother—regardless of whether Keely was estranged from her or not—he couldn't tell her the truth about himself.

He looked over the table at her, as if seeing her for the first time. Although from very different worlds, they'd both faced circumstances they couldn't control and were forced to grow up quickly. His heart ached for her because he knew exactly how it felt to be abandoned by your mother, the one person who should love you unconditionally.

He reached out, clasped her hand in his. Their gazes met and held. Seeing the vulnerability beneath her dark lashes, he had the sudden urge to pull her into his arms again. Protect her from sadness and harm. Fix everything in her life that needed fixing.

After they finished eating, they made the ten-minute walk to her shop. He enjoyed being with her and used every excuse to touch her, keeping his hand on the small of her back most of the time. Stepping onto the curb.

Guiding her around a break in the sidewalk. At one point, when two young girls weren't watching where they were going and almost ran into them, Toryn cupped Keely's shoulder and drew her out of their path. She flashed him an easy smile, lighting up the dark corners of his heart. She was uncomplicated and enjoyed his company.

When they rounded the final corner, Keely hesitated, then frowned.

His hand tightened on her shoulder. "What's wrong?"

"Our sandwich board sign." She pointed down the street. "It should be on the sidewalk below that blue awning, but it's not there."

When they got to the shop, shards of glass covered the pavement, glittering like raindrops in the moonlight. A black hole gaped in the window, obliterating the name of the shop that was painted on the glass—Sisters something. A broom lay on the sidewalk, as if someone had tried to sweep up the mess, then changed their mind.

Keely gasped and clamped a hand over her mouth.

Toryn drew his blade. The window above the door had been broken as well. The point of entry. The latch on the worn brass door handle pressed easily. The door was unlocked.

"Stay out here," he ordered. Without waiting for her response, he pushed it open.

The small bell overhead chimed out a misplaced cheery welcome. He stepped over the threshold and into the darkened shop.

Even without lights, he could tell the place had been vandalized. Books and loose papers were strewn over the floor, shelves were tipped over, and tiny bottles that held oils and lotions were scattered everywhere.

"Oh my God," Keely said from right behind him. "My books."

Toryn sighed. He hadn't really expected that she'd wait outside for him, but it was worth a try.

"Stay put. I'll check the rest of the place." He did a quick but thorough search of the premises, including the small apartment upstairs. No one else was here, and there didn't appear to be any other damage.

When he returned to the main floor, Keely was struggling to raise an overturned bookshelf.

"The place is clear," he said, rushing to help her. "Looks like this is the extent of it."

She ducked her head away from him, swiping a hand hurriedly over her cheek. "Thank you, Toryn."

He started to reach out to her again but then thought better of it. He couldn't let himself get emotionally attached to her any more than he already was, but before he could pull back, she touched his hand lightly. A soft, feathery touch, like a butterfly.

Damn.

"I...I don't know what I would've done without you," she said, chewing on her lower lip, probably to keep it from trembling. "I can't imagine coming back to this... alone. The last time it happened, Becca was here."

His eyes narrowed. "This has happened before?"

She nodded. "A few times. We're prime fodder for the more militant protesters given who our father is and that we used to be on their side. So in a way, I guess we deserve this."

She'd mentioned that her father was a minister with a popular online show whose Internet ratings brought in lots of ad revenue. Toryn nodded, even though he didn't understand much. He came from a world with castles, warriors and horses, not computers, electricity and cars. About the only thing he understood was that her father was a powerful religious man.

"You were a kid when you protested with him," he said brusquely. "I hardly call that being deserving of this kind of retaliation."

She didn't look convinced. "I don't know, Toryn. I'm not sure that I would've changed my mindset about Talents if I hadn't become one. I had a really hard time accepting the fact that I was a freak. I'd—"

"You're not a freak, Kitten," he said softly. Her gaze flashed to his as if she were trying to decide whether to believe him. "You're not."

She swallowed, looked down at her hands. "I became the very thing that I grew up despising. Both of us did. I don't know what I would've done without Becca. I'm not sure I could've gone on without her."

He exhaled slowly. The world wouldn't have been the same without Keely in it.

Despite Keely believing this was the work of protesters, he wasn't so sure. Not with the timing of what happened to her sister. He'd be willing to bet that Reaux was behind it somehow. In his experience, the power hungry would often do things to demonstrate their might and rattle their sabers.

He didn't want to think of what would've happened had she been alone and come upon the bastards while they were still here, but from now on, he'd do everything in his power to keep her safe.

While she gathered up papers and re-shelved books, he boarded up the windows with some plywood he found in the alley.

"So the name of your shop is Sisters Books and…what?"

"Books and Fortunes. Although the fortunes part is more marketing than anything else."

He quirked a brow. "How so?"

"Becca and I don't actually read fortunes. It's more like making thought suggestions, although to be honest with you, she's much better at it than I am."

"When you're done, maybe you can show me. Give me a demonstration."

She laughed and said she'd love to.

After he finished hammering the last nail, he stood back to check his handiwork. "That should hold for now."

"I can't thank you enough for your help," she said as she rested her hands on top of the broom. "This would've taken me all night by myself."

The place wasn't completely put back together, but at least it was better than it had been. He brushed his thumb over a smudge on her cheek. "No thanks necessary, Kitten. I was happy to do it."

They exchanged another heated glance and he felt himself getting hard.

"Is there somewhere you can stay until the windows are replaced?" The words came out low and raspy. "A friend? A relative, maybe?"

Shaking her head, she stepped away from him and straightened a few items on a nearby counter. "No, there's just Becca and me. I'll be fine though."

He thought about this latest Iron Guild mission and how he'd considered using Keely to get to Reaux. The thought disgusted him now. She was an innocent young woman who didn't deserve to be thrust into danger like that. He'd figure out another way to take the bastard down.

Up until now, his hatred of Reaux had been strictly professional. The man was a threat to the Cascadian people and it was Toryn's duty as an Iron Guild warrior to neutralize that threat.

But that was before he met Keely. Now, it felt personal.

"Then I will stay here with you until it is fixed."

CHAPTER SIX

"Can I get you something to drink?" she asked, handing him a pillow and blanket. They didn't have a spare room, so the couch in the reading nook in the back of the shop would have to suffice. His large, imposing frame seemed to fill the entire space. How would she be able to sleep knowing he was on the floor below her?

Grinning as if he knew what she'd been thinking, he settled down on the sofa and stretched his long legs out in front of him. "Got any Irish whiskey? The good stuff?"

"Darn. I'm afraid I'm fresh out. I do have some top-shelf wine, though."

"Excellent."

She returned a few minutes later with two

mismatched wine glasses and a bottle of strawberry wine.

She unscrewed the top, poured him a glass, and when she handed it to him, her fingers accidentally brushed his. The echo of his touch shot up her arms and gave her goose bumps just like it had before.

She took a seat next to him on the couch, trying as hard as she could not to snicker like a twelve-year-old boy with a whoopee cushion. Surely he knew that this wine was as cheap as they came, didn't he?

Without a whiff or a swirl, he knocked back the entire thing in one gulp.

"Bloody hell," he sputtered, putting the empty glass on the library table beside him. "That stuff is awful."

She laughed at his reaction—just what she'd hoped it would be—and took a sip. It wasn't *that* bad. "A little sweet maybe," she admitted. "It's Becca's."

A knot of worry twisted in her stomach again at the thought of her sister. She hoped nothing happened between now and tomorrow to prevent her from coming home. Then, all Keely had to do was convince her not to go back. They could move away. Start up fresh somewhere else, somewhere far away from Davin Reaux. She'd heard that things were better for Talents down in Portland, and she'd always liked it there anyway.

As if sensing her tension, Toryn took her glass, set it

next to his, and motioned for her to turn so he could massage her shoulders.

He lifted her hair aside and placed his hands on her skin.

Mmmm.

They were warm, heavy and strong. She closed her eyes and focused on his deft fingers kneading her tight muscles. Inch by inch, the tension from the past few days began melting away.

It felt good being with him like this. Safe. Relaxing.

"So what do you do, Toryn?" she murmured, her eyes still closed. "Other than rescuing women and doing minor construction projects."

"For one thing, I didn't rescue you." His tone sent delicious shivers down her spine. "You did that all on your own. I was just the lucky fellow who happened to be at the right place at the right time for that kiss."

Lucky was right, but she was the one who was lucky. Her face heated at the memory of that amazing kiss, and she wondered if a second one would be as electrifying as the first. She had a pretty good idea that it would be.

She coughed awkwardly. "So what were you doing when I…uh…ran into you?"

It took a moment for him to answer, as if he were trying to decide what to tell her. "My associates and I were trying to figure out a way to infiltrate Reaux's network. He's a hard bloke to track down. And then there's the matter of those bloody Psychic-Talents."

"Your *associates*?" she asked.

Again, he hesitated. She was going to ask if he was in law enforcement, but then she remembered how he'd acted in the alley. It had been very clear to her that he hadn't wanted to speak with the Night Patrol.

Her shoulders tightened beneath his strong, steady grip. He wasn't talking about organized crime associates, was he?

"So what's *your* issue with Mr. Reaux, since we seem to have that in common?"

"All I can tell you is that I'm part of a group trying to prevent him from hurting and taking advantage of innocent people. He and others like him commit all kinds of atrocities. We're trying to put a stop to it."

So he wasn't in some rival faction vying for the same turf, she thought with relief. As far as she was concerned, anyone trying to keep Mr. Reaux from doing any more harm was one of the good guys. But a group that operates outside the scope of the authorities...?

"You mean like mercenaries?"

"Yes." The finality in his tone told her he was done discussing the subject.

He continued massaging her neck and shoulders, finding the knots and working them out. Jeez, it felt good. Too good, she thought as she imagined his hands on other parts of her body.

"You're not put off by someone with a Talent," she said. "Why is that? Does that mean *you* have one?"

His hands stilled on her shoulders. She started to crane her neck around to see his expression, but he pointed to a bookshelf in front of her. A book moved. And then another.

She jumped. "Oh my God, you did that? That is so cool!" She twisted around, looking up into his magnetic gray eyes. "Why didn't you do that earlier when we were cleaning up?"

A corner of his mouth turned up. "I didn't want to freak you out. Plus, I try not to use it too much. I'm sure you understand."

Yes. She knew exactly what he meant.

"Speaking of Talents…" Something glinted in his eye. "Say I'm a customer in your shop. I come back here, sit down and—" He held out his hands. "Do you read my palm? My tea leaves?"

"Not exactly." She shifted and took his hand, flattening out his long, calloused fingers. "Please keep in mind that I'm not that good."

"Let me be the judge of that."

"Okay," she said with a smile. She thought for a moment, then tilted her head and concentrated, feeling the energy sizzling down her arm.

His brows knit together, then he burst into laughter, a deep rumbling sound that had her laughing as well. "Did you just implant the thought that I want a brownie?"

"Yep."

"I thought so. I can practically smell it." He let out a low whistle. "Ye could play some mean-ass practical jokes on folks."

"Well, I can't do anything beyond simple suggestions of things that already appeal to you. Unlike Becca, who can get people to imagine all sorts of things. That's how our parents found out about us, actually." She paused, thinking back to that horrible time. "We were at a youth retreat up in the San Juans with some high school friends. There was alcohol. Becca and I— Well, it was my stupid idea. We ended up doing some things we shouldn't have, which exposed both of us."

She let out a controlled breath. What a nightmare it had been. The fights, the yelling. The therapy. As if being a Talent meant you had mental issues.

He slipped his fingers between hers and caressed her knuckles with his thumbs. There he was again. Sensing her stress and doing something to alleviate it. His touch was simple yet extremely intimate, and it sent molten heat straight to her core.

She bit her lip, trying to quell the need rising in her body.

He continued to stroke the delicate skin on the back of her hands. "So the question is, do you have any brownies? For some crazy reason, I've got a craving for them."

She smiled sheepishly. "I'm afraid not."

"Seriously?" He pulled her onto his lap, and she let

out a surprised laugh. With her hands resting on his shoulders, she was sitting eye to eye with him. And straddling his legs.

His broad hands splayed over the curve of her hips, and something devious lit up behind his eyes. It both thrilled and excited her, and she found herself wanting to see just how naughty he could be.

He cocked an eyebrow at her, as if he had read her thoughts. "You have the nerve to implant a brownie craving into my head, but you don't have any?"

"I might have some chocolate chips." Lame, yes, but she wanted to come up short, just to get his reaction.

"Are you kidding me?" he asked with mock outrage.

"Why? Are you frustrated now?"

"Very frustrated. And it's completely your fault."

She had her hands on his shoulders, breasts not far from his face as she waited in anticipation.

"And now, Kitten, I'm afraid you must pay the price."

He gripped her hipbones in her most ticklish spot and dug in his thumbs. Shrieking with laughter, she tried to push away from him. She bucked her hips and arched her back, but he was too strong and too determined to keep her right were she was.

Which, if she were being honest with herself, was exactly what she wanted. She was wildly attracted to his man.

When she felt the steel rod of his erection pressing up against her core, he stopped tickling her.

They were both breathing hard. Some of his raven hair had slipped from the knot at his nape, and dark need reflected in his eyes. She imagined she had the same look in her eyes. She wanted him. So damn bad.

He possessively gripped the back of her neck and brazenly ran his other hand over her breast, sending shivers down her spine.

His nostrils flared slightly. "Ye've been a very bad girl."

CHAPTER SEVEN

Toryn knew he was going to have a hard time controlling himself. Every fiber of his being thrummed with the need to possess her. To mark her as his own. The first night when they kissed, he'd been so shocked by the whole damn thing that he simply went along for the ride. A very enjoyable ride, but it had not been one of his making.

This time, however, he was the one in control. And he intended to make the most of it.

He pulled Keely to him and his mouth crashed over hers. With his tongue pressing along the seam of her lips, she opened for him, eager and welcoming, just like he knew she would. She tasted sweet, like strawberry wine, and purely female.

He slid his hands over her luscious curves, enjoying how her supple flesh yielded to his touch. He tugged off her shirt to reveal a lacy black bra with a tiny red bow on each wide strap. And when he peeled off her jeans, he found a matching set of panties.

The soft, creamy skin of her cleavage bounced and flattened against his chest as he unhooked her bra and removed it. Cupping her voluptuous breasts in his hands, he grew even harder. She seemed to sense it too because she ground her hips against him.

"So beautiful." He dipped his head and took a nipple into his mouth while teasing the other into a hard nub with his thumb.

She hissed and arched into him, then gave a soft kittenish mewl that drove him even more insane. His erection strained painfully under his clothes, but he continued to suckle and flick her with his tongue.

"Oh God, Toryn. Please…" She fumbled with his belt buckle and slipped a hand into his pants, her cool fingers closing around his length.

He groaned at her touch, needed to be inside her.

He stripped off her panties, shoved the books aside and lifted her onto the table.

"Toryn, my books."

"We're not going to hurt the blasted books," he growled.

He grabbed a condom from his wallet and quickly sheathed himself, then he spread her knees and stepped closer. His balls felt heavy against his upper thigh as he slipped two fingers past her pink folds and found her slick and ready for him. He wiggled his thumb against her clit and she cried out, her inner muscles clamping around his fingers.

Was she on the verge of an orgasm already? Curious to see how responsive she was to him, he leaned over her, drew a nipple into his mouth, then curled his two fingers and stroked deep inside.

Her whole body trembled and tightened. He kept pressing, stroking, licking, bringing her higher and higher. She cried out his name, her climax crashing over her. He stilled his hand, though he didn't withdraw it, and watched as she came undone around him.

———————

Keely's breath came out in short, needy gasps as she clutched the edge of the library table. She'd literally just had the best orgasm of her life, and from the looks of it, she was going to have another.

A few minutes ago, when she first laid eyes on his impressive male form jutting out at her, she'd felt a rush of liquid heat between her legs. He'd been very pleased at how easily she'd come for him then, and now he was ready for round two.

Toryn gripped the base of his latex-covered cock. "Kitten, spread your legs wider for me," he rasped, expecting her to do as he said.

She had no idea how he'd come up with that nickname, but she did as she was told.

"Yes, that's it," he said, his eyes dark with desire as he stared at her sex. "Perfect."

She was surprised at how good his praise made her feel. She was independent, accustomed to being the one in control, but oddly enough, although she was submitting to him, she felt even stronger, more powerful.

Almost immediately, she felt the blunt head of him slip past her folds. She held her breath, waiting for his hard thrust and hoping it wouldn't be too uncomfortable at first, but the edge of the table restricted his movements. Gripping her hips, he lifted her up and slid her slowly onto this thick girth instead.

"Holy Fates, Kitten," he said through clenched teeth. "Ye are so bloody tight. I'm afraid I am not going to last very long."

"Me either. You feel so good inside me."

A smile tugged at the corners of his lips. She could tell this pleased him immensely.

Buried all the way to the hilt, their pubic bones touching, he remained still for a moment to give her body a chance to get used to him inside her. He nuzzled her neck, caressed her breasts.

Up until now, she really hadn't been into sex. Couldn't figure out what all the fuss was about, actually. She'd had a few boyfriends, had a few orgasms, but they hadn't been anything special. The boyfriends *or* the orgasms. They were nothing she couldn't accomplish on her own—without any of the accompanying hassle.

But this?

Now she was starting to understand. She just hadn't been with the right partner, one who cared about her pleasure before his. It wasn't like her to have sex with someone she just met, but something about him called to her on a deeper level. She'd felt so lonely for such a long time. An outcast. But Toryn seemed to understand her and made her feel as if she finally belonged.

He braced a hand behind her on the table and began rolling his hips, sliding his iron-hard erection back and forth against her highly sensitized clit. She was vaguely aware that a book had fallen to the floor, but at this point, she didn't care. She arched into him as a delicious heat surged through her like wildfire, starting at the tips of her fingers and toes, working its way inward until all the focus was on where they were joined.

He felt so good there, his cock thick and demanding inside her, awakening a raw, savage need that she never knew existed. She clung to his shoulders, her hips meeting each of his powerful thrusts.

"You're so tight around me," he said, his voice ragged with desire. "I can feel how close you are. Let go, Keely. Can you do that? It's time for me to take over."

Let him take over.

Four simple words.

With everything in her life spiraling out of control, being with Toryn was like holding onto a rock. A lifeline. She felt safe with him. Protected.

And she didn't want it to end.

"Okay," she whispered, "take over for me, Toryn."

He let out a low, possessive growl. Grabbing a handful of her hair, he pulled her head back and kissed her hard, with a passion she'd never experienced before.

She dug her nails into his back, wanting to put her mark on him.

Then she cried out his name for the second time as a huge climax splintered through her.

"That's it, Kitten. That's it."

His next thrust went even deeper, demanding access to every part of her.

He groaned, his whole body shuddering. She felt him pulse over and over inside her, intensifying her pleasure even further. If not for the condom, he would've filled her to the brim with his potent seed. Her inner muscles clamped down on him, holding him there, uniting them together.

CHAPTER EIGHT

avin Reaux didn't like to be disappointed.

Not by his friends. Not by his business associates. And certainly not by the people who worked for him. He glanced at the champagne glass on the adjacent table and could feel his anger rising.

How hard was it to keep the damn thing filled?

He cleared his throat to get someone's attention. The blonde between his legs stopped what she was doing and looked up.

"Not you, sweetheart. Keep going." He patted her head and she continued.

A brunette—a girl named Cheryl, he believed—was over near the window. She hurriedly wiped the blow from her nose. "What can I get you?" she called.

He ground his teeth together. "First of all, come over

here when you're speaking to me. No one likes to hear someone yell across the room."

"Oh yeah, right." She rose and sauntered over.

He'd let the *yeah* slide…for now. There were too many other things to work on at the moment. "And second of all, this isn't a fast food restaurant." He cocked his head expectantly.

She blinked a few times, looking flustered, then it dawned on her. "I…I'm sorry. How may I be of assistance…*sir*?"

"There you go. See how much better that sounds?" He raised his brows and waited for her to agree with him. "The clients like that. It tells them that your sole purpose is to serve their needs, whatever they may be."

"Yes, of course, sir."

"Now, can you tell me what's wrong here?"

She looked down at the girl. "Is she not doing it right?"

"No, that's not it. Keep looking."

She scanned the table. "I…I don't know, sir."

Did she have the IQ of an ameba? But she was cover model beautiful and that was what mattered the most. "Look at the glass."

"Oh my goodness," she said, her eyes widening. "The glass. I'll fill it right away, sir. Was that the Cristal?"

He gripped the armrests to keep from slapping her across the face. It wouldn't be good to present a bruised girl to the clients. *Of course he'd been drinking the fucking*

Cristal. And if she were in tune with his needs, she would've remembered.

"Yes," he said through clenched teeth.

Closing his eyes, he leaned back and tried to relax, pay attention to the sweet thing between his legs. He was semi-hard at best and probably wouldn't ejaculate, but it still felt better than not having a blowjob.

There was a knock on the door.

He let out a long sigh. "That's enough," he said to the girl with his dick in her mouth. He pointed to the drug-laden table near the window. "Go help yourself now."

He rose and headed to the door, not bothering to cover himself up. It was just his assistant; she'd seen him like this before. "This better be important."

"Oh, it is," Iris said, breezing into the room with an efficient, no-nonsense clip to her step. Her chin-length silvery hair was pulled neatly off her face with a thin black headband. She glanced over at the two naked females near the window and the two passed out on the bed. One of them was finally stirring. "I wouldn't have bothered you if it wasn't important."

"What is it then?" He grabbed a piece of bacon from a platter on the table.

"I just got off the phone with Freddy Ubinov."

Again? The Russian billionaire had called him every day this week. "Did he not get the catalog? What did he think of the girls?"

"No, he got the catalog," Iris replied, tapping a stylus

on the edge of her tablet. "That's not the problem. Seems he's looking for a certain kind of girl and didn't see her listed."

Davin let out an exasperated sigh. "What the hell kind of girl is he looking for? We've got almost a dozen for him to choose from. All beautiful and all have a Talent."

He'd specifically chosen the girls not just for their looks, but also for their particular Talents that could be used to heighten the sexual pleasure of their partners. He wasn't the only one who ran a Talent sex trade club, but he was one of the best. No one put their girls through as much rigorous training as he did. And it paid off. His auctions attracted some of the biggest clients, and he made a helluva lot of money doing it.

He glanced at the beautiful sword mounted above the mantel, its jewel-encrusted hilt glinting in the light. A precious antiquity acquired during a recent raid he'd financed into Cascadia. One—no, two men had died bringing the thing back through the portal. There was a big market for Cascadian treasures, and at auction this sword would likely fetch as much, if not more, than one of these girls.

"He's looking for a female with a very specific look." Pushing up her glasses, she consulted her tablet. "A redhead with big breasts."

"Redhead? Did he not see Rita?"

"Too skinny. Not edgy enough. Said if that's all we have, he and his boys aren't coming."

"Fuck." He strode to the window. If Freddy didn't come, it would be disastrous. They were some of the biggest whales on the guest list. If anyone else caught wind of it, they could change their minds, too.

Davin grabbed the glass of champagne and drained it. "A redhead with a Talent *and* huge tits? We don't have anyone like that."

A blonde curled up on the sofa caught his attention. He'd forgotten she was there. Wasn't she telling him something before about some redhead she knew? *A Talent?*

With his open robe streaming behind him like a cape, he strode over to her and patted her on the cheek. "Hey, Betty, wake up."

The girl mumbled something and wrapped her blanket tightly around her.

"I'm talking to you." He grabbed the edge of the blanket and jerked, and the naked girl spilled onto the floor with a clunk.

"Sir, careful," Iris said. "She's one of our most valuable girls. With her looks and her unusual Talent, we're getting all sorts of interest. She's going to fetch a very high price."

"She's a goddamn junkie is what she is," he bit out, pinching the bridge of his nose. No one understood how hard his job was—finding the girls, making sure they were ready. He didn't have a lot of time to make miracles happen. The VIP event was right around the corner.

He turned back to the blonde, who had pushed herself to a sitting position and was rubbing her head.

"Betty," he said softly.

The girl looked at him, blinking a few times before she responded. "It's Becca."

Whatever. He leaned over and stroked her messy hair. "Tell me more about this sister of yours."

CHAPTER NINE

Take over for me.

Keely's simple statement replayed in Toryn's head as he ran up the steep stairs of the hillclimb, sweat dripping in his eyes. She'd chosen to give him control last night, but he wondered at its broader meaning.

He'd woken early, thinking he would slip out for a run while Keely slept, but she was already awake. She'd nuzzled in close, her breasts pressed against his chest, which had been all the encouragement he'd needed. He'd pushed her onto her back, and they made love without a word, the only sounds were the rustle of the sheets and the soft moans she made when she came.

It had been incredible to wake up next to that beautiful redhead, her heart beating inches away from his. And after they made love, she'd molded her soft curves to his hard edges again. He'd assumed she would fall back asleep, but she got up, too, and asked him to drop her off down at the rowing club. Then they could come back and have breakfast.

He took the stairs two at a time, arms and legs pumping until he reached the top where he turned around and came back down. When he called Sean last night and told him he was staying here, the man hadn't asked any questions, which Toryn appreciated. He hated having anyone up in his business. Sean left the Jeep near the shop and was going to have one of the other warriors pick him up.

Over and over Toryn ran the stairs, his mind working as hard as his body. He thought about the hint of sadness in Keely's eyes and how he ached to chase the shadows away.

Not only was she strong, compassionate and smart, but her body, with its luscious curves, seemed so finely tuned to his. Every look from her, every touch, made him want to bury himself inside her again. He was getting aroused right now just thinking about it, which wasn't good when all he was wearing was a pair of thin gym shorts.

Take over for me, she'd said.

He cursed under his breath.

Would she still have said that if she knew who he really was? A barbarian soldier from the other side of a portal?

Guilt sliced through him like a blade of hand-forged Balkirk steel at this deception of his. If she knew the truth, would she still feel the same way about him? Would she still have said that? Or would she cast him out, angry to have shared her bed with a man she thought was a terrorist?

Or worse still—would she be afraid of him?

Hell. If he were being honest with himself, was he even capable of trusting another human being with his heart? He'd been too naive once, trusting someone who broke his heart, so he'd vowed never to let that happen again.

When he was finished, he headed back to the rowing club located on a narrow channel of water near the Fremont Bridge. The bridge wasn't used for cars any longer—it had been too badly damaged in the earthquake years ago—but evidently the city engineers thought it was safe enough for the rowing club and some industrial buildings.

He arrived in time to see Keely carrying the scull in from the water, her long red hair blowing in the wind from the lake.

"How was your workout?" he asked, helping her lift the lightweight boat onto the rack.

Her cheeks were rosy from the cool morning air. "It was good. I haven't felt like coming down here for a long time. My parents keep their boat moored on the other side of the Locks." She pointed down the channel to her left. "What about your run?"

"Grueling," he admitted, redoing the knot of hair at his nape as they walked to the Jeep. The cool morning air felt good on the back of his neck.

"I can only imagine. You couldn't pay me enough to run that hill."

"Really?" One side of his mouth quirked up in a smile. "You wouldn't run it for a hundred credits?"

Stepping in front of him, she turned around and walked backwards. "Nope."

"How about five hundred?"

"Let me think about it." She put her finger to her cheek. "Nope. That's not enough either."

He chuckled. "That's too bad, because I'd really like to see you sweaty and out of breath."

"I can think of a few other activities I'd rather do to get me sweaty." She lifted an elegant brow and gave him a sultry look, but she wasn't watching where she was going and almost tripped on a crack in the pavement.

His arm shot out, pulling her close. "Careful," he warned, staring at her luscious lips. "You could hurt yourself." They continued walking—him forward, her backward.

The tip of her tongue darted out. "Not if you're here to catch me."

He felt himself growing hard. Again. When they got back to her place, he'd make love to her in the shower, he decided—her hands splayed against the tile and that sweet ass in front of him.

Guilt that was never far from the surface clawed at him again. He needed to tell her the truth about who he was. He couldn't keep dragging it out. It wasn't fair to her. She deserved to know. Plus, he was proud of what he did—it was a big part of his identity, and he wanted to share that part of himself with her.

But he had to be prepared for her to leave, and he wasn't ready for that just yet.

Not that he was falling for her or anything. Nope. Not going to happen.

Something behind him drew her attention and she frowned.

He turned, following the direction of her gaze.

Two men in dark clothing were behind a bridge piling near the rowing club. One slipped off what looked to be a heavy backpack, while the other man paced and glanced around nervously in the thin morning light.

"What do you think they're doing?" she whispered.

"I don't know. Doesn't look good."

There'd been a car bombing a few weeks ago. The authorities blamed it on Cascadians, of course, but there were those within the Iron Guild who believed the army was actually behind it. After all, it benefitted them to keep the tension high between the two worlds. You couldn't exactly justify a big military presence without an imminent threat.

"Wait here. I'll go see."

She scoffed. "I'm coming with you."

Jaw set sternly, he placed his hands on her shoulders, holding her in an iron grip. "No, you're not, Keely. Not this time."

The men were now hunched over a small black box with wires sticking out. As the Guild's explosive expert, he had no doubt what this was.

"Fuck. It's a bomb." He shoved her in the opposite direction. "Run."

Keely thought Toryn was right behind her until she got to the corner, threw a glance over her shoulder and saw that he was halfway back to the bridge. He'd run *toward* the men who were setting the bomb, not away.

She came to a screeching halt, sheer terror racing through her body. What was he thinking? It was two against one, and they were most likely armed. The authorities should be handling this, not Toryn.

She patted the pocket of her sweatshirt and remembered she'd left her cell phone in his Jeep. She'd once lost a phone in the lake while rowing, so she'd stopped taking it with her when she went out.

Damn it. She needed to call the police.

She spun around, looking for someone—*anyone*——and gasped with relief when she spotted an elderly man walking a tiny dog. Dashing over to him, she asked if he had a phone.

He frowned, his bushy gray eyebrows pulling together. "What?"

"A phone! Do you have a phone?"

"You want to use my phone? Well, yes. I have one back at my apartment."

Oh my God, could he talk any slower?

He pointed a gnarled finger in the general vicinity behind him. All she could see were empty warehouses. He must live a few blocks away. But she didn't want Toryn out of her sight.

A maroon sedan was pulling into the rowing club parking lot. They had to have a cell phone, but in case they didn't, she needed to have all her bases covered.

"Can you call the police?" she asked the old man. "Tell them there are two men down at the base of the bridge. My...my boyfriend thinks they're planting a bomb."

"A bomb? Oh my gosh. That's terrible! Yes, yes, of course." The man hurried off.

She turned to sprint toward the car but hesitated when she saw Toryn. He was crouched behind a stack of pallets about thirty feet from the men and was reaching out a hand in their direction.

What was he—?

Suddenly, both men jumped back from the box as if they'd been hit by something, but she couldn't tell what.

Had Toryn done that? Used his Talent, maybe?

One man was covering his head with his arms as if he were expecting an explosion. She froze, holding her breath in horror. Toryn was too close. If it exploded, he'd be seriously injured…or worse.

When nothing happened, the men stepped back to the box. Then one of them reached down and jerked something out. Looked like wires. The other man shoved him and gestured wildly. He was clearly angry with his partner about this.

She glanced at the car. Crap. It wasn't pulling into the rowing club. It was driving back out of the lot on the far side.

It was then that Toryn chose to step out from his hiding place and sprint toward the men.

They jerked their heads up in unison, but Toryn was lightning fast. One man swung a fist at him, but he easily dodged the punch and sent the guy skidding back on his haunches.

The other man reached into his coat, drew a weapon and pointed it straight at Toryn.

"Noooooo!" she screamed, anguish ripping a hole in her chest. This couldn't be happening.

She braced herself against the coming bloodshed, but…wait. It looked like the assassin was saying something to Toryn. Then, a moment later, the gun flew from his hands, the trajectory arching upward as if it had been thrown, and it flew into the water about thirty feet from shore.

The man looked down, dumbfounded at his empty hand. It appeared as though he might charge Toryn. There was a flash as Toryn pulled out his blade.

And then she heard it. Sirens. Dozens of them.

Looking to the left, she could see the flashing lights on the other side of the channel. The bombers heard it too and took off running in the opposite direction. Her knees felt suddenly boneless, and she grabbed the chain link fence to steady herself.

It was over. Toryn had confronted the men and scared them off. But more importantly, he was unharmed.

A moment later, he was at her side. "Come on," he commanded roughly, his hand enclosing around her upper arm and pulling her in the direction of his Jeep.

She stepped in front of him and wrapped her arms around his waist, not wanting to ever let him go. She couldn't believe she'd nearly lost him. The thought was almost unbearable. And then she thought about how he'd gone down there to confront them on purpose. "Oh my God, Toryn, you could've been killed." She punched her fists on his chest in frustration. "Why did you do that? We should have left an anonymous tip with the authorities and let them handle it."

He shook his head, urging her forward. "It wouldn't have done any good."

She took a few steps then stopped. "Why?"

"Because it's happened before, Keely. Countless times. Those men were soldiers."

"Soldiers? You mean Cascadian terrorists?"

Toryn's eyes darkened as the sirens grew louder.

"Come on. We've got to get out of here. This is a military operation."

"Toryn, you're not making any sense. How do you know all this?"

He pressed his lips together into a thin line. "The bastard with the gun told me, confirming what I already knew. Said the army wanted the bridge blown up and told them to make it look like the work of Cascadians."

Her head was spinning. None of this made sense. "And why would he tell you that?"

"Because he was a Pacifican soldier. And because *I'm* a Cascadian."

CHAPTER TEN

oryn fucked up. And he wasn't sure what he could do to fix things.

As soon as they arrived at Sisters, Keely rushed across the floor of the shop to the stairs leading up to the apartment.

"Keely, wait," Toryn said, following closely behind. "We need to talk about this."

She ignored him, kicked off her sneakers at the bottom of the stairs and started up. He grabbed her hand and stopped her.

"Please, Keely, let me explain. Don't shut me out like this."

She spun around, hazel eyes blazing. "What's there to explain? I thought you cared about me, and then you drop *that* on me?"

Her words felt like a slap across the face. She

despised him. He disgusted her. He thought about letting her go and leaving. Walking out the door behind him and not coming back. After all, if she were truly repulsed by the fact that she'd been sleeping with one of those *terrible barbarians from Cascadia*, then why would he want to be with her?

And yet, something told him that maybe her anger was because she was hurt.

"I do care about ye," he said, not bothering to hide his accent. He didn't want to lay his heart bare, but he was going to have to if he wanted to get through to her. "I never expected to develop feelings for ye, Keely—I tried so bloody hard not to—but when I did, I was afraid that if ye learned the truth about me, you'd kick my ass to the curb and want nothing more to do with me."

"So you lied."

He raked a hand through his hair. "I wasn't completely honest."

"There's a difference?"

She tried to pull away from him, but he wouldn't let her go. "Listen to me, Keely. I—"

"Why would you think I'd do that?" Her cheeks were two bright spots of color. "Do you think I'm that shallow? That a person's birthplace or nationality is a checkmark on a list of acceptable traits for my ideal man?"

"I wanted to tell ye, but when I learned that your family believes my people were responsible for the bomb that injured your mom, I was— Well, I didn't know how you'd react."

Anger simmered behind her eyes. "You've been nothing but wonderful to me and yet you think I'd be incapable of accepting you? Jeez, Toryn, I'm the one who's used to not been accepted."

"I'm an Iron Guild warrior and we *are* coming over here to fight your army, so it would be logical for ye to abhor me. Blame me as a proxy for what happened to your mom. I know I probably would, if I were in your shoes."

"Seeing what I did today," she said, rubbing a hand over her face, "I doubt that your people were even responsible for my mom's accident." She crossed her arms over her chest. "I don't think you trusted me to keep your secret. Is that it? Did you think I would go to the authorities?"

His gaze snapped to hers. "Of course not. I had to be careful at first, sure, but it became clear to me early on that ye would never do something like that."

"Then why, Toryn?" Her voice was soft. "Why not tell me tell me the truth?"

He looked away, his heart pounding in his ears. Why was she pushing him like this? Hadn't he told her enough? He didn't want to admit to her one of his darkest fears, but if he didn't, he would lose her. "It's just that...I've been betrayed by people I've cared about, so trusting comes hard for me."

"What happened to you?" she asked gently.

"I was a young warrior and fell for a girl I thought loved me back. Turned out all she wanted was to use me to get through a portal and make a life for herself here. Without me."

Keely was quiet for a moment. "And you thought I would do the same thing? Hurt you like she hurt you?"

"I…I didn't know."

At first he thought she was upset, but then she leaned down, cupped his face in her hands and kissed him, her lips so soft and tender against his. "I'm falling for you, Toryn, so I sincerely hope that you can learn to trust me."

His heart thudded in his chest at her admission. "I'll *try*, Kitten," he said thickly. "That's the best I can do for now. Okay?"

She was silent for so long he feared that it *wasn't* okay.

"As long as you'll try," she said. "That's all I can ask."

Then he swept her into his arms and carried her up the stairs.

They made love in the shower, just as he had fantasized. After washing away the sweat and stress from the morning, he splayed her hands on the tile wall and took her from behind, holding onto that sweet ass of hers as he buried himself inside her. Rivulets of water ran down her back and dripped from her full breasts, making it easy for his hands to slide over every luscious curve.

He brushed her wet hair aside, nuzzling the back of her neck right above the butterfly tattoo on her shoulder, and chuckled with satisfaction as she shivered. As his cock slid through the liquid heat of her tight channel, the pressure in his balls increased. Soft moans escaped her lips as he fondled her clit and touched the juncture where his body disappeared into hers. She cried out his name as she came, her inner muscles clenching around him, milking his release. A moment later he joined her, his hoarse groans echoing off the tile walls while molten pleasure pulsed out of him.

When they were finished, he pulled out of her and discarded the condom. She turned to face him, slipping her arms around him and pressing her body close. Her cheeks were flushed, her wet hair hanging in thick strands around her upturned face.

She'd never looked more beautiful.

"That was a much better start to the morning, don't you think?"

"Mmmm," he rumbled against her ear. "I agree. Much better."

A short time later, they sat against the headboard, legs entwined, sharing a delicious breakfast scramble that

Toryn had made. She hadn't felt much like eating, but he'd insisted.

"Is it true that those with Talents have Cascadian blood in them?" she asked, trying to keep her mind off the fact that Becca should be here this afternoon. *If* she'd been telling the truth. *If* she wasn't high and forgot. *If* Mr. Reaux let her go.

He nodded. "While not every Cascadian has a Talent —it often skips generations—many are gifted."

She took a bite that he offered her and chewed it thoughtfully. "Why is it just over there? Why aren't there more Talents over here?"

"Have you heard of the Obsidian Wars?"

She frowned. "It sounds vaguely familiar, but I couldn't tell you why."

"Doesn't surprise me," he said grimly. "If a historical event isn't passed down to subsequent generations, it's as if it never happened."

"Can you tell me?"

Toryn set the plate aside and she settled against his chest. His voice rumbled in her ear as he spoke.

"The Obsidian Wars happened many years ago, stemming from a jealousy between brothers. Two of the brothers had Talents, one did not. Each had his own kingdom. After their father died, there was a power struggle based on jealousy and greed. The brother without a Talent coveted what he didn't have and eventually war broke out. Finally, after many years of bloodshed, the Three Fates stepped in and divided up the worlds with portals, separating the brothers. Although that stopped the war, it didn't stop Pacificans from trying to seek the magic of our world."

"Most people here believe Cascadians come through the portals to terrorize us," she said, rubbing her hand absently over his washboard abs.

"That is the prevailing thought, yes, but the opposite is actually the truth."

"So our army goes over there? For what reason?"

A dark, brooding look crossed his face. "They are trying to find the *fata-magic* and want to bring it back here to use."

"*Fata?*"

"From the Fates. The magic that resides inside many Cascadians that gives us our Talents."

Her eyes narrowed. "So if the magic is *in* you, how do they, the army, get it?"

"They come for our children."

Keely's hand stilled. "*What?*"

Toryn shook his head sadly. "They take the wee ones and bring them over here in the hopes that they'll develop a Talent that can be later exploited."

"And what happens to the parents in Cascadia?"

Anger flared in his eyes and he exhaled roughly. "They kill them."

She felt like throwing up. Families being torn apart,

people killed. "And what's Davin Reaux's role in all this?" She almost didn't want to know.

"In return for financing some of the army's missions, he gets to keep the bounty. Precious artifacts from our abbeys and monasteries that he can sell over here on the black market for huge sums of money."

"Precious artifacts?"

He nodded. "Handcrafted swords and weapons. Jewelry. Religious relics. Everything disintegrates during a portal crossing, unless it's iron-based or encased in an iron receptacle. Those who carry these objects through usually die though."

Her mouth dropped open in shock. "Someone dies? Who'd sign up for that?"

"Simple," Toryn said. "The army doesn't tell them. The poor young recruit who carries dense metal objects through the portal has no idea he's going to die as soon as he gets to the other side."

CHAPTER ELEVEN

CHAPTER ELEVEN

The window repairs had just been completed when the bell over the shop door rang. At first Keely thought one of the workers had left something behind and was coming back to get it, but when she looked up, it was her sister walking through the door.

"Becca!" She rushed over and tackle-hugged her.

"Whoa," her sister said with a laugh, extracting herself and setting her handbag—one that Keely had never seen before—on the counter. "You'd think I've been gone for months instead of a week."

Without removing her sunglasses, she waltzed into the shop, bringing with her a heavy dose of perfume as her gold strappy heels clicked on the wood floor. She wore an off-the-shoulder sheer top, skinny jeans, and gold bangle bracelets that clinked with every movement —all new.

"I've been worried sick about you," Keely breathed, leaning against the counter for support. "Thank God you're back."

Becca flicked a hand in front of her face as if she were flicking away Keely's concern. "What are you talking about? I called you and told you I was fine."

Keely was surprised by her sister's haughty tone. This wasn't like her. Becca could be bossy and impatient sometimes, just like any older sister, but she'd never sounded like this before. Keely caught a whiff of cigarette smoke and stale alcohol as she walked past. "What's with the shades?"

"They're new. All this is new," Becca said, holding out her arms in a game show hostess sort of way.

Keely scowled. "Yeah, I noticed. And most people take off their sunglasses when they're inside. Especially when the sun isn't out."

Becca put a hand to her forehead. "Stayed up late last night partying and drinking, that's all. I woke up with a wicked hangover and my eyes hurt."

Keely followed her upstairs. Becca's thick blond hair, while looking good from the front, looked unwashed from behind.

"Want me to turn on the shower?" she asked. In this old building, it always took a while for the hot water to kick in. "Do you need some Tylenol? I can grab you some from the medicine cabinet."

"Thanks, but I'm not staying long." Becca opened her dresser and started throwing some clothes into a suitcase. "Can you grab my makeup bag while you're in there?"

It felt as if someone had just punched her in the stomach. Sure, Becca had told her on the phone that she was only coming by to pick up a few things, but Keely had hoped she'd changed her mind. "You're not staying? Why? Where are you going?"

"We've discussed this already." There was that note of irritation again.

"No, we haven't."

"I told you, the other girls and I are staying out on a private yacht."

What the hell? "A private yacht? You told me nothing about this, Becca. This is the first I'm hearing about it."

"I can't help it if you don't listen to me when I talk. I distinctly remember telling you all about it on the phone the other day." She let out an exasperated breath. "We're working a big VIP event and this is part of our training. There are some very important people coming in for this, and every detail needs to be perfect."

"You're staying on Mr. Reaux's boat?" She seriously felt as if she were getting sick.

"Jesus, Keely, it's not a boat. It's a private yacht. Big difference. We've all got our own staterooms. We're going on a dry run tomorrow, out to international waters." She held up a string bikini. "Do you think I should bring this?"

Okay, giant red flag. Massive.

"Becca, listen to me. Heading out to international waters with a man like Mr. Reaux is just plain dangerous. You shouldn't go back there."

Her sister laughed. "That's crazy talk. You've never met him. He's a very wonderful and generous man."

"What? Like he's your sugar daddy now?" Keely made a sound of disgust. "That's gross. He's Dad's age."

"I don't need to listen to this. You don't know what you're talking about." Becca continued shoving things into her bag.

Keely tried another angle. "What about the shop? I can't run this place without you. You know that. How are we supposed to pay the rent if we're not bringing in any money? It's due next week."

"Seriously, Keely. You worry too much. Mr. Reaux is taking care of all of that for us. The rent is paid for the next few months."

Keely was stunned. "He's paying the lease on Sisters?"

"Yeah, isn't that great of him? I told you he's really generous. In fact, when I told him about you, he said he'd love to meet you, too."

Keely swallowed hard. "What for?"

Her sister shrugged. "I don't know, silly, but my guess is that he'd be interested in hiring you as well. He only hires Talents for certain positions and the pay is amazing."

Horrified that Becca had been talking to Mr. Reaux about her, Keely shook her head.

"Well, you should let me introduce you and then maybe you'll stop being such a spoil-sport. Listen, nothing bad's going to happen. He's on our side, don't you understand? He would never do anything to hurt us."

Keely walked over to the window and glanced out, trying to calm her racing heart. Becca was talking as though she'd been brainwashed or just joined a cult. Could she not see what was going on?

"Becca, take off your glasses."

Her sister sputtered. "Why?"

"I want to see your eyes."

"So you can accuse me of being high? Oh my God, Keely! Stop being so…so judgmental." She zipped up her bag and threw it over her shoulder. "You're starting to sound just like Mom and Dad. And frankly, I've had enough of that kind of bullshit. I don't need it from you as well."

"I'm not being judgmental," Keely said. "I'm just worried about you, that's all. Trust me, Mr. Reaux isn't the wonderful person you think he is. He's a bad, dangerous man, and you're a fool to think otherwise."

Becca swung around to face her and lifted up her sunglasses. Her eyes were rimmed with red and the dark circles underneath were so pronounced they looked like bruises.

"You know nothing about him," she said through clenched teeth. "Nothing. So shut your mouth."

"Well, for your information, someone broke out a few windows in the shop the other day."

"And you think Mr. Reaux had something to do with it? *Please.*" Becca rolled her eyes and headed down the stairs. "Protesters, Keely. That's what they do."

Or a not-so-subtle message that they needed Reaux's protection.

Keely debated whether or not to tell her she'd been by the club only to be chased by Reaux's men, but in the end, she decided not to.

"When will you be back?" she asked, following her sister down to the shop.

"Not 'til after the party."

"And you're going to be gone for a few weeks? For God's sake, Becca, I can't keep the shop open without you. You know that. Why didn't you run any of this past me first?"

"I did," Becca said, biting off each word. "And you were okay with it."

In her delusional drug-induced memory, maybe.

Becca stepped around her and reached for the door. "You should be happy that I'm not implanting a suggestion in your mind right now that you should come work the party, because I totally could, you know."

The little hairs on the back of her neck stood on end. "You wouldn't dare."

"Of course I wouldn't. I'm just teasing." Becca winked and then adjusted her sunglasses as she walked out the door. "I'm not that much of a bitch."

"Have you gone completely insane?" Konal stared at Toryn as if he'd just sprouted horns. "Rickert will have your head if you bring an outsider to an Iron Haven."

"What do you call Sean then? He's not an Iron Guild warrior."

"Sean's situation is different. I know you don't like the guy, but he has the permission of the Magistrate and the Council to be working with the Iron Guild. Your girlfriend, on the other hand, does not."

"I don't do girlfriends," Toryn bit out. Truth was, Keely was much more than that, but he sure as hell wasn't going to admit it.

Konal lifted an eyebrow. "Yeah, I know, which is why I'm so confused right now."

"There's nothing to be confused about. She's in danger from the man we're after and has nowhere else to go. Until it's safe for her to go home, she's going to be staying with me."

"Sounds like a girlfriend to me," Konal muttered under his breath. "Bottom line is, you do not have permission to take her to the Iron Haven. Doing so would expose Iron Guild secrets to an unauthorized Pacifican and risk your standing with the Guild. You've worked too hard for that."

Damn the rules.

He knew his friend was right, but it didn't make it any easier to swallow.

"Besides," Konal added, "if you did that, Rickert would be well within his rights to have you flogged."

Their leader was not into any rule-bending since he got his command back. He'd been punished and temporarily stripped of his command for bringing an unauthorized enemy soldier—Neyla—through a portal, so the guy did everything by the book now. Which was irritating.

Toryn inwardly flinched. Even though it had been many years, he remembered exactly how the sting of the whip felt on his bare skin. At the orphanage, it was the headmaster's favorite form of punishment. After a particularly brutal flogging, he'd run away and wound up training for the Warrior Games, a competition where young men competed in various speed, strength and endurance events for the chance to join the Iron Guild.

"You've always been a rebel, Toryn, I get that. But even a rebel has to follow some of the rules or there will be hell to pay."

"Then I'll take her to that old hunting cabin on the

river. It's no longer used as a rendezvous point now that the Iron Havens are operational."

"You're going to take her to that shithole? Ha. Good luck with that. The last time we were there, we had to knock down a huge wasp nest inside. It was not pleasant." Konal folded his arms over his brawny chest. "So what's with this girl, anyway? You seem…pretty attached to her. And that's not like you."

It was true that he kept himself emotionally detached from the women he slept with. And he was good at it. Never spending more than a night or two with each one.

But with Keely, things were different. He ached to have her in his bed night after night, watching the desire in her eyes turn to molten lava as she came, holding her in his arms, talking about things that mattered and feeling like she understood him. Although the risk of betrayal weighed heavily on him, she was chipping away at his self-control.

If he could get past his trust issues, was a future together even possible? Sure, a few of the other warriors had made it work, but could he and Keely? The truth remained that they came from two different worlds, and unlike his friends' women, she'd grown up with personal, deep-seated beliefs that his people were barbaric assassins. Despite her assurances, their differences could ultimately tear them apart.

"She's going through a rough patch right now and

has nowhere else to turn. I'm just helping her out, that's all."

She was strong and capable on the outside, but on the inside, she was sensitive and vulnerable. Maybe no one else saw her like that, but he sure as hell did.

Konal sighed. "Let me talk to Rickert. I can't make you any promises, and he's probably going to have my head for even asking, but I'll explain to him that you're falling for a Pacifican girl with a Talent and that you're concerned about her safety. That's something the guy can relate to."

Toryn gritted his teeth but didn't argue. If that's what it would take for Rickert to agree, then so be it.

Konal continued. "Maybe it'll make a difference to him knowing she's got the *fata-blood*. That's got to count for something, right?"

As Toryn drove back to New Seattle, he thought back to that conversation on the stairs when Keely told him she was falling for him.

It would shatter her heart when—if—they parted ways. And the thought of hurting her twisted his gut into knots.

CHAPTER TWELVE

"You can take it off now," Toryn said gruffly. Keely reached up and removed the blindfold, a requirement set forth by the other warriors. She blinked a few times as she peered out the Jeep's windshield. Even though it was dark outside, it took a few moments for her eyes to adjust.

She had zero clue where they were. No one outside of the group he worked with could know the location of this place, and they obviously took that very seriously. She and Toryn had left New Seattle earlier in the day and been four-wheeling over rough terrain for the past several hours. And she'd had the blindfold on the whole time.

The headlights illuminated part of an old building surrounded by tall fir trees, but then Toryn turned off the engine and everything went dark again.

"Listen," Toryn began, turning in the seat to face her. "Most everyone is fine about you being here, but there might be one in particular who…well…could be a little standoffish."

"Great. Thanks for warning me ahead of time so that I could change my mind."

She never should've let him talk her into coming here, but the minute she told him what Becca said, he'd made a few phone calls and they were soon on the road. Before that, she'd already decided to close up shop for a while. The thought of who was paying the rent made her sick to her stomach. It didn't feel like it belonged to her anymore. She wasn't sure what she was going to do, but she sure as hell didn't want to owe Mr. Reaux anything.

She stepped out of the vehicle and was met by a blast of cold air. She shivered, pulled her scarf tighter around her neck and grabbed her duffel bag. The sounds of crickets and frogs echoed in the darkness along with the far-off howl of a coyote.

"Here. Let me take that," Toryn said, coming around the front of the Jeep and grabbing her bag.

Tucking her hands into her pockets, she looked at the building in front of them.

So this was an Iron Haven. The headquarters for Toryn's mercenary group. She couldn't say that she was particularly impressed.

It seemed to be some sort of rundown resort with

boarded up windows, tangles of blackberries climbing up the sides and thick layers of moss on the roof. Off to the right was a cluster of canoes covered in weeds, relics from an earlier era, which probably meant there was a lake or river nearby.

Movement in front of the building caught her attention. A dark-haired man wearing what looked to be a kilt stood in the doorway. His arms were drawn tightly across his chest and he had a stern, unwelcoming expression.

Yep. He definitely looked standoffish.

Toryn put an arm around her shoulder as they walked to the entrance, and he introduced her to Rickert, the Iron Guild warrior leader.

The man nodded, said a brusque hello, then stepped aside so they could enter. He didn't seem at all pleased that she was here.

When they crossed over the threshold, she was surprised at what she saw. The condition of the inside did not match the rundown condition of the outside. In here, a major renovation was underway. There were sawhorses and drop cloths. Cans of paint and stacks of drywall. Rather than smelling old and musty like she'd expected, the resort smelled of fresh paint and new wood.

They were in a large foyer, two stories tall, with a freestanding river rock fireplace in the center and what looked to be the original guest registration desk to the left. She heard the sound of muffled voices and laughter in the distance.

"Toryn," Rickert said, "I'd like to speak with ye. In private."

"Of course."

Just then, a very attractive blonde woman entered the foyer from the hallway on the left. Casual yet stylish, she wore black leggings, a purple cashmere sweater and a beautifully made hand-knit silver shawl.

"Rickert, honey," she scolded, "they're probably starving. Let them eat first." She turned to Keely, held out her hand and introduced herself. "I'm Neyla. You must be Keely. It's so nice to meet you." She lowered her voice. "It always takes him a while to warm up to new people. In fact, when we first met, he was planning to throw me in jail."

Keely liked the woman immediately.

Neyla hooked her arm in Keely's and led her in the direction from where she'd come, leaving Toryn and Rickert to bring up the rear.

"How was the drive?" Neyla asked.

"Long," Keely said with a slight grimace. "But I slept most of the time. Not being able to see made me tired, I guess."

"Blindfold?" Neyla asked. When Keely nodded, the woman gave her an apologetic smile. "Figures."

The sounds of voices and laughter grew louder as

they walked down the hallway. Neyla pushed open two huge double doors at the end.

"Welcome to the *activities* room," Neyla said. Given the way she phrased it, Keely assumed she was referencing some sort of joke.

A man and a woman doing a jigsaw puzzle on the coffee table rose, grabbed their wine glasses, and came over to say hello. They introduced themselves as Vince and Zara. There were three people near a table covered with food. Toryn introduced them as Asher, Olivia and Konal.

Konal grinned. "Keely, it's very nice to meet you. Glad to have you here. Toryn's told me a lot about you." Then he laughed heartily. "Not really. Getting info out of him is next to impossible."

So this was Toryn's best friend. She shook his hand and smiled.

"I hear you two met over a kiss," the man named Asher said. "You must be one helluva kisser for him to bring you home."

Olivia elbowed him.

"What?" he said, frowning.

"You said you were going to be on your best behavior."

"I am," he retorted, a feigned look of hurt on his face. "That was a compliment."

There was a hint of a smile on her lips. "Right. Now be good."

Asher lifted a brow. "Watch your tongue, Lass, or there'll be payback later."

Soon, Keely was sitting at the table with a large plate of food in front of her. Rickert had corralled Toryn and led him to the other side of the room.

"Toryn tells me you live in the Circus District," Olivia said, taking a sip of her wine. "And that you're a Talent."

Keely nodded. "My sister and I run a shop down there." It felt strange to admit to people she hardly knew that she had special abilities. Strange, and yet kind of liberating at the same time. "Or, I should say, we used to run a shop there. I had to close it down. Temporarily until...well, until this whole mess with my sister gets sorted out."

"Whereabouts is your shop?" Olivia asked, slanting a glance at Asher. "I dated a guy once who ran one of those underground fighting rings in the area."

Yeah, she'd heard about a few of them. "It's a few blocks up from the waterfront. Near Yesler."

Olivia nodded. "Isn't there a really popular mobile coffee cart around there? I used to work at a wine and coffee store downtown, and I remember hearing about it."

"Circus Coffee? Yeah, but I'm not sure what's going to happen since their popular barista went missing."

Asher overheard them. "Was she a Talent?"

"Yeah," Keely said, spearing a cherry tomato from her salad. "The last person she was seen with is the same guy who hired my sister. At least I've seen Becca, but—" She thought about the bruises under Becca's eyes. "As far as I know, no one's seen or heard from Hanna."

"I'm sorry your sister is messed up with Davin Reaux," Olivia said. She cocked her head in Asher's direction. "These guys have been trying to infiltrate his network for awhile now and having a hell of a time."

Keely looked down at her plate. "I'm worried about her, too. But what makes it even harder is that I didn't have anyone to turn to. Until Toryn…"

She felt the heat of his stare. She lifted her eyes and saw that he was watching her from across the room where he and Rickert were talking.

"Well, now you have us," Olivia said brightly.

Asher, his arm around Olivia, agreed.

"Both Neyla and I know what it's like growing up in Pacifica and then discovering you are a Talent," Olivia said.

Neyla gave her a warm smile. "It's not easy. But you're among friends here."

"Definitely," Olivia said, nodding. "I hope you'll have a chance to visit Cascadia sometime. Talents aren't feared or exploited there. They're treated like they have a gift. Just like an athlete, artist, or musician over here."

Keely hadn't spent much time thinking about what the world was like on the other side of a portal, but if it was anything like the easy rapport she was having with these two women, then she was intrigued. She could almost see herself going over there, setting down some roots.

"Speaking of talents," Keely said, eyeing Neyla's knit shawl. "You didn't happen to make that, did you? Because it's gorgeous."

Neyla brightened. "Yes, I did. Thanks."

"I knew it," Keely said, absently touching her own pale blue infinity scarf. "I've never seen a stitch like that."

"Sounds like you're a knitter yourself. I'd be happy to show you how to do it. It's really easy once you know the trick."

Keely sighed. "If I could live in a yarn shop, I would. When Becca and I were trying to come up with a concept for our shop, I lobbied hard for Sisters Yarns and Fortunes, but Becca doesn't knit or crochet, so in the end we decided to go with books, and you can't really go wrong with books."

Toryn returned to the table a few minutes later and sat next to Keely. Rickert had wanted to know what safety precautions he'd taken on the way up here. On no uncertain terms was Keely allowed to go outside unaccompanied. If and when they did go out, she was to be blindfolded before crossing the Esmerelda line. She was not allowed to know where the Iron Haven was located or how to get here.

Yada yada yada.

Rickert was nitpicking everything.

Konal had been right. The Iron Guild leader was doing everything by the book now that he had his command back. He wanted to prove to the leadership in Cascadia that they'd made the right decision putting him in charge again.

"I understand ye are able to shield your thoughts from Psychic-Talents," Rickert said to Keely.

Toryn slipped a hand over the back of her chair and absently stroked her shoulder with his thumb. It was nice to see her fitting in so seamlessly with his people. Maybe the two of them weren't so different after all.

She shrugged. "I didn't know that one of those men was a Talent. I just wanted them to continue running past me, that's all."

"Interesting." Rickert took a swig of his beer. "And ye were able to shield Toryn's thoughts from them as well, otherwise they would've realized he was a threat."

She nodded.

"Think ye can do it again?"

Toryn's head snapped up. What was the guy implying?

"I'm not really sure," Keely answered hesitantly. "Maybe."

Toryn glared at Rickert. He knew he should be

respectful of his leader, but he had a feeling things were about to get ugly. "You're not saying what I think you're saying, are ye? Because if ye are, the answer is a flat-out no."

Rickert seem unfazed. "What if she can get a few of us past those body guards? We'll be able to get to Reaux and—"

"What the bloody hell, Rickert?" Toryn said, aware that he was raising his voice to his leader. "I'm getting a serious case of whiplash here. Ten minutes ago, you're lecturing me about bringing her, and now ye want her to be a part of this mission? It's treacherous enough for a trained warrior."

Keely put a hand on his arm. "Toryn, please. Let's talk about this. I'm willing to do anything if it'll help get my sister back."

He jerked away from her. "No. It's too dangerous."

"She's my sister," Keely said through clenched teeth. "And this is *my* decision."

Even though she was making his blood boil, Toryn knew he was on the verge of losing this argument. "What if someone recognizes you? That red hair is a dead giveaway."

"They didn't see my hair," she said. "I had a hood on, remember? But I can wear a wig."

"What if you're not able to maintain a shield for long? You shielded the two of us for, what, a total of ten seconds?"

"She can practice, Toryn," Rickert said, butting his nose in where it didn't belong. "And if it turns out she can't maintain it, then we won't use her. It's that simple."

Toryn thought about how he'd intended to use her at first as well. And it made him sick now. She was so much more to him than a means to an end.

"This is her call, Toryn," Rickert reiterated. "No one else's."

Toryn dropped his fork with a clatter and pushed up from the table. Who the bloody hell did Rickert think he was? Of course she would want to help her sister. But that didn't mean she should.

Konal stepped in front of him. "You don't want to do that."

Toryn scowled at his friend. "He wants to send Keely into the mouth of the dragon, and you expect me to be okay with that?"

Konal lowered his voice. "We're just talking, okay? Throwing out ideas."

"Yeah? Well I'm throwing that one away."

"Hey, uh, you guys?" Sean was on the other side of the room, looking at his computer screen. "One of the news sites is reporting that another woman from the Circus District has gone missing. They're saying she's a Talent."

"Oh my God," Keely said. "Who?"

"Hold on, let me see." He paused to read more of the article. "Oh sorry. It says here that the authorities believe it's a domestic dispute and has nothing to do with the missing barista. Apparently, *this* woman had been having an affair with a guy whose wife just found out about it."

Keely looked relieved that the disappearances weren't connected, which made Toryn relax in turn. The less stressed she was about the situation, the better.

Zara had been picking up empty bottles from that side of the room and now peered over Sean's shoulder. "Ha. It's Birdie Lyons' vlog," she said to Vince.

"Who's that?" Toryn asked.

"She thinks she's a journalist," Vince snapped. "But she's a fucking joke who cares only about ratings and clicks."

"The only thing newsworthy about that woman's show," Zara said, "are the outlandish outfits she wears."

Toryn must've looked confused, because Vince added, "It means you can't trust a thing she says. Otherwise you'd believe that Zara was a prison bunny —" he said with air quotes "—who associates with the deadly, dangerous and deranged."

Zara flashed Vince a knowing half-smile and rubbed her flat stomach. "Well, I do associate with dangerous men who knock me up, so at least that part is true."

"What's the missing woman's name?" Keely asked. "I wonder if I know who she is."

Sean turned back to the screen. "Um…Verla Martinez."

"What?" Keely gasped in horror. "That's wrong. That can't be her."

"Did she work at a tattoo parlor?" Sean asked almost apologetically.

"Yes. Oh my God." Keely's hands were shaking. "I...I can't believe they're saying it's not connected."

"You know her, Kitten?" Toryn asked, reaching for her hands and sandwiching them between his.

"Verla is a friend of mine. She's my tattoo artist," she whispered hoarsely. "And she wasn't having an affair with a *man*. That's bullshit. Verla's gay."

While everyone else crowded around the screen to read the article, Keely turned to Rickert. "Tell me what I need to do to prepare."

<h1 style="text-align:center">CHAPTER THIRTEEN</h1>

Keely spent the next week working with one of the trainers who specialized in helping the warriors hone their Talents, an elderly man brought over from Cascadia whom everyone simply referred to as the Grey One. She wondered what they called him when he was younger. It was grueling work, mostly mental, and after they were finished with the lessons, she tumbled into bed each night completely exhausted.

She already knew basic self-defense, having taken Krav Maga a few years ago, but she brushed up on her skills and incorporated some basic knife drills. She hoped she wouldn't have to use any of it, that getting the warriors past the psychic guards would be enough.

After much trial and error, the Grey One had come to the conclusion that the only people Keely could reliably shield were her and Toryn. The rest were spotty, at best. After learning that, Toryn had wanted to scratch the mission altogether, but Keely refused.

In the end it was decided that Toryn and Keely would go into the club alone, while the rest of the warriors would provide support from a safe distance.

"Oh my God, you look gorgeous," Neyla said, putting the finishing touches on Keely's attire. "Not bad for such short notice."

"Can I turn around yet?" Keely asked. "I want to see what strip club chic looks like."

"Hold on." Neyla pulled and tucked a few things while Olivia did something with her hair. "Okay, now you can look."

Keely whirled around and looked in the full-length mirror. Her breasts spilled over the top of a black corset and a full-length black skirt draped flatteringly over her curves. "Holy crap," she breathed. "I hardly recognize myself." She touched the wig, an electric-blue bob that came just past her chin. "And this dress, it's simply gorgeous. I've always wanted to wear a corset."

Neyla beamed. "Glad you like it, but it's all very functional as well. The corset has a hidden panel for your knife. That way, if they're having guests go through metal detectors, you'll be fine because the corset has metal boning. Even if they pat you down, they'll just think the knife is another piece of boning." Neyla continued to scrutinize the fit. "Your dress is dual purpose. You've got this semi-sheer black fabric for the overskirt but underneath is a pair of slim silk trousers. That way, if you need to make a fast getaway, you can kick off your shoes, pull off this outer skirt and go."

To complete the look, she wore bright red lipstick, silver earrings and studs, and false eyelashes.

"I love this tattoo," Olivia said, pointing to her arm.

"Thanks. It's new." She ran her fingers over the script. "It's from my favorite poem. Verla did it for me." A lump formed in her throat at the thought of her friend.

Olivia nodded thoughtfully. "It's lovely," she said, giving Keely a hug. "I know you'll find them. Toryn is the best there is."

When Toryn stepped into the room a few minutes later, she nearly had a heart attack. The man was freaking gorgeous. He wore a well-tailored black tuxedo that emphasized his broad shoulders and narrow hips. His thick raven hair was neatly captured in a low bun. She seriously wanted to take him back upstairs and ravish him.

"You look beautiful, Kitten. Seriously stunning." He was eyeing her cleavage as if he wanted to take a bite.

She'd never worn a corset before...but she was pretty sure this wouldn't be the last time.

"Something's wrong, Toryn."

They had just made it past the registration table at the entrance of Aphrodistic and were standing in front of an elaborate floor-to-ceiling bar, one of several around the place. Sean had worked his magic and gotten them onto the guest list, along with fake identification and papers.

Toryn looked around warily. House music boomed through the speakers and neon lights flashed from the DJ booth. Several raised platforms contained dancers in micro-bikinis with chains and collars around their necks. People were everywhere. The place was packed.

"What is it?" he asked, not finding the source of her concern.

"Those two bodyguards back there who checked us in? They weren't psychics. Or if they were, they're not very good. It was nothing like the drills that the Grey One put me through."

"Maybe you're stronger now and a little blip doesn't register any longer."

She shook her head, the blue hair of her wig skimming her jawline. The color was so startling and different from how she normally looked that it caught him off-guard every time. A good thing, actually, otherwise his gaze would automatically drop to her breasts spilling over the top of that corset. Hell. If not for that beacon of blue hair, he'd have a perma-hard-on from staring at her gorgeous figure all night.

"I don't know," she said. "It doesn't feel right. If this party and auction is everything we've heard it will be, shouldn't there be more of them around? I mean, the night I met you, they'd had at least one Psychic-Talent on duty."

A waitress in a skimpy leopard costume glided by. He grabbed two glasses of champagne from the tray and handed one to Keely.

"No thanks," she said. "I can't afford to lose any mental focus." She tried to give it back but he refused.

"Keep it. You'll fit in better if you've got a cocktail or a champagne flute in your hand."

He inclined his head in the direction of the upper level that looked down on the main floor. "Let's go up there to get a better view of the place."

He took her hand and forged a path through the crowd. They skirted around a couple where the man was unfastening the woman's bodice. One of her breasts popped out just as they passed and the man groaned. Another couple was kissing at the bottom of the stairs, and two women on a nearby bench were doing the same thing.

Sexual displays of affection were commonplace in Cascadia, but not over here. Things were bound to get crazier as the liquor flowed and the night wore on.

When they got to the glass landing suspended halfway between the two floors, Keely's hand tightened around his.

"It's him!"

He stopped, sliding his hand to the small of her back. "Who?"

"The same Psychic-Talent who was chasing me. I can sense him."

"Where?"

"Upstairs," she said, chewing nervously on her lip. "But he's coming this way."

"No worries, Kitten. You've got this." He stepped her backwards until they were against the railing. Tilting her chin up, he stroked his thumb along her jaw and watched as the tension in her face disappeared. Her arms slipped around his neck and he felt the now-familiar sizzle of her Talent's energy as she shielded their thoughts.

"You look beautiful in that wig. The whole outfit, actually." He nuzzled her neck and she shivered. "But then, you could be wearing a burlap sack and I'd find it impossible to keep my hands off of you."

"Really?" she asked, arching a brow. "Because I love your hands on me."

Out of the corner of his eye, he saw the man making his way down the stairs, heading straight for them. He was speaking into a tiny microphone clipped to his ear. Toryn shifted protectively in front of her.

"That can easily be arranged." He dipped his head and kissed her, slipping the tips of his fingers into her corset and finding her nipple right there. Damn. If this thing slipped any lower, her breasts would be on display for anyone to see. A wave of possessiveness swept over him.

She is mine.

Keely moaned into his mouth, and he felt himself get harder.

"He's…he's gone," she said breathlessly.

"That's nice," he said without stopping. Her nipple was erect between his fingers.

"Toryn, if you don't stop, I might…"

"You might what?" he asked, pressing the length of his cock against her hip.

"I might—oh God—I might come. We cannot…do… this…here."

Was she serious? She moaned softly. Holy Fates. She was. "Why not?"

"We're surrounded by people."

He pushed his thigh between hers, forcing her legs apart, and squeezed her nipple harder. "Tell me to stop and I will."

Her fingers dug into his shoulders. "Toryn, please."

"Please what?" he whispered against her neck, pressing his leg to her core. "Stop?"

She gave a little gasp, and her whole body trembled in his arms.

When it was over, he chuckled under his breath and brushed a blue strand of hair from her face. "Holy Fates, Kitten. That was hot."

Keely's cheeks were flushed. "Yeah, it was."

When they got to the second floor, they threaded their way through the throngs of people and headed toward the railing. It was definitely an older crowd up here, Toryn thought. More men with gray hair and paunches, several with trophy wives or girlfriends hanging on their arms.

From their vantage point, he could see a narrow hallway on the first floor behind the DJ booth. It was cordoned off with a burly man in a tuxedo monitoring the comings and goings.

"There," Toryn said in a low voice. "That hallway."

She nodded. "It looks like a good place to start."

But before they could head back downstairs, the volume of the music came down and a voice boomed out.

On a large monitor above the stage was a balding man with a round, jowly face wearing a tuxedo. "Welcome to Aphrodistic. Where all your sexual fantasies, sadistic or otherwise, come true."

"That's him," Toryn said under his breath. "That's Reaux."

Keely grabbed his arm. "Why is he on the monitor? Why isn't he here in person?"

"Before we get tonight's erotic cabaret started," Davin Reaux was saying, "I'd like to say a special hello to our VIP guests, watching from a remote live feed." He lifted his glass in a toast.

Everyone looked around, trying to figure out whom he was referring to.

For the first time, Toryn noticed that the second level where they stood didn't wrap the entire way around the club. On the other wall, six huge monitors were hung in a grid—three rows of two. One by one the monitors lit up as the people on the other end activated their feeds. First was 2B, where three businessmen in suits were lounging on black leather couches. They were being served by three beautiful naked women.

The man next to Toryn elbowed him. "The guy in the middle looks like the founder of Gupsie. Glad I don't own stock."

Toryn didn't know what that was, so he just nodded tersely.

3B was the next monitor to light up, revealing a group of young men who were panning the camera, holding up their beers.

"Looks like they're on spring break," someone behind him said. "Hey, isn't that Jason Jones from the Portland Eruption?"

"Where?" said another voice.

"The one in the back getting a blow job."

Soon, all of the monitors were lighting up. Men in suits, tuxedos and caftans surrounded by beautiful women. Every monitor except 2A. People started to go back to what they were doing, assuming that 2A was empty or wanted to remain anonymous, when the monitor suddenly flashed. It showed one man standing in front of the camera, legs shoulder-width apart, hands crossed over his chest. With a thick neck and broad, boxy shoulders, he had the body of a professional wrestler. At his side was a voluptuous redhead on her knees. Blindfolded with her hands tied behind her back, she had a collar around her neck, and the man was holding the leash.

Keely gasped. "Oh my God, that's her!"

He scanned the monitors for a blonde girl. There were several. "Which one?"

"The girl in 2A," she said, clutching his arm for support.

Toryn looked again. "Are you sure? I thought your sister was blonde."

"She is," Keely choked. "They must have colored her hair. But that's Becca all right. See the tattoo on her shoulder? It's a butterfly. Same as mine. We've got matching tattoos."

The music picked up tempo as dread coiled in his gut.

Those were video feeds. Which meant that Reaux, and more importantly, Keely's sister, could be anywhere.

CHAPTER FOURTEEN

What was she going to do now?

Keely was in the restroom trying to clean off the mascara under her eyes with a paper towel. She'd cried in Toryn's arms when she realized that Becca wasn't at the club but at an unknown location with a sadistic asshole who had her on a leash. What had he done to her? What was he *going* to do to her? She couldn't bear to think about what her sister was going through. All she wanted to do was bring her home. And see Reaux brought to justice.

The music got louder as the door opened, and a man walked in. She bristled and looked away.

Damn co-ed washrooms.

She hated looking into a mirror—redoing makeup, fixing her hair, or in her case, wiping off tears—if random men were using the sink next to her. For God's sake, the tampon machine was right next to the condom dispenser.

Not wanting to run into a Psychic-Talent security guard on her own, she hurried to get out of here. There was something about being with Toryn that gave her more confidence in herself and her abilities. If she'd known that the restroom was co-ed, she would have made him come with her.

The door opened and closed again. Bracing herself to see another creep, she turned around and was shocked as hell to come face-to-face with Verla. She wore a tiny French maid costume and the same collar as many of the other waitstaff.

Before she could say anything or throw her arms around her friend, Verla gave a little shake of her head and slipped Keely a napkin. Then without a word, she went into one of the stalls and locked the door behind her.

Thirty minutes later, just as the note instructed, Keely and Toryn were waiting in the alley behind the club, the same alley where she'd climbed out the window a few short weeks ago.

The door opened and Verla emerged carrying two white plastic trash bags.

"Verla, oh my God, what happened? The news vlogs reported you went missing. You're not working here, are you?"

Verla barked out a harsh laugh. "Not voluntarily."

She fingered the collar at her throat. "It's a shock collar. Can you believe that? Like we're dogs or something. Get too far away, and you'll be in the worst pain you can imagine."

"Can we cut it off?"

"With what? Do you happen to have a spare pair of tin snips lying around?"

Hardening his jaw, Toryn turned away from them and punched a few buttons on his phone.

"Do you have any idea where Becca is?" Keely asked.

"I'm not sure," Verla replied, "but when Iris, Mr. Reaux's executive assistant, was in the other day, she got a call from a delivery service. Apparently, they were having trouble delivering something to one of the islands. I heard her spell it out for him. I'd never heard of it before. I remembered it because it was such a strange name."

"What name?"

"Cluck Island, I think. Have you ever heard of it?"

Keely took a step backward and clapped a hand over her mouth. She'd been to Cluck Island many times. Her father used to hold religious retreats there. They'd get there by boat and park in a slip at the tiny marina.

Toryn stood on the bridge next to Keely, training the

binoculars on the small island looming ahead of them. Another thirty minutes and they'd be there.

Keely navigated her family's thirty-seven-foot cabin cruiser like an expert through the chilly waters of Puget Sound. Although it had been years, the marina hadn't changed the access code, nor had her father changed the spot where he hid the boat key.

After they cut off Verla's tracking collar and took her home, the warriors had met up at Sisters Books and Fortunes to plan their next move. When Keely told them she knew how to get to the island on her family's boat, it was decided that all the warriors would come.

The engine didn't turn over at first, but Toryn rattled a few wires and it started right up.

"How did it get the name Cluck Island?" Olivia asked Keely.

"Years ago, a ship ran aground on the island with a cargo of live chickens. Since there are no natural predators except for eagles, the chicken population grew."

"Are they still there now?"

She shook her head. "No, not since my father started holding retreats on the island. They rounded them all up."

Asher hadn't been crazy about Olivia coming with them, but as a Healer, her Talent might be necessary. Vince and Zara were out on the bow. Vince's Talent, being able to find portals, wouldn't be put to use, but Zara's—the ability to cloak herself—might. Vince hadn't wanted her to come either. They had a son back in Cascadia staying with grandma, and they'd recently found out they were expecting another child. But Zara insisted, saying she couldn't sit back like an invalid while innocent girls were being hurt.

Konal stood off by himself while Sean stayed inside on his computer. He'd pulled up the current charts as well as the weather forecast. They were expecting some higher swells, but a storm warning hadn't been issued. At least, not yet.

Keely dropped anchor on the other side of the island from the main lodge because there was less chance of being spotted. She doubted any of the VIPs or Reaux would be taking any nature walks through the woods. That wasn't why they were here.

They broke up in teams. Because of Zara's Talent, she and Vince would go in cloaked to find Becca and bring her out. The rest of the warriors would take up positions outside the compound, ready to take action.

Knowing Keely couldn't stay put and not be involved, Toryn asked her to be in charge of rowing the group onto shore.

"Wait for us here."

"But—"

"Keely, I'm serious." He cupped her face in his hands

and gave her a hard kiss. "This is a dangerous mission. Iron Guild warriors only. Your job is to stay here and get us back to the boat. We'll find your sister. I promise."

CHAPTER FIFTEEN

*P*atience was definitely not one of her virtues.

Hands shoved into her pockets with her collar turned up to block the icy wind, Keely paced back and forth along the rocky beach in front of the dingy.

"Be ready for us," he'd said.

The crescent moon was high in the sky above the *Dee-Light,* named after her mother, which was bobbing on the choppy waves in the tiny inlet.

"I *am* ready for us," she said aloud to herself, her words carried away in the wind.

She wanted a future with Toryn, couldn't imagine what her life would be like without him. She wanted to wake up next to him tomorrow, next month, ten years from now. He'd been there for her when no one else had, and she wanted him to truly accept that she'd never betray him. He'd been through a lot, just as she had, and the thought of hurting him was almost unbearable.

As she waited for him, she walked along the beach, the same beach that had held the fateful bonfire that changed everything. Although Becca had been a senior in high school and Keely just a sophomore, she'd always let her little sister tag along. Keely had always tried hard to fit in with Becca and her friends—a little too hard.

The prank had been Keely's idea. She'd figured Becca would say it was stupid and childish, but she hadn't. So, fueled by the poor judgment of too many beers, they teamed up and implanted the suggestion that Cory and Jeff should kiss. Thinking back on it now, it really was a hilarious prank. Two macho, completely-hetero-to-the-point-of-homophobic football players kissing on the lips in front of the bonfire. To say they had not been happy about it was an understatement. The shit pretty much hit the fan after that.

She picked her way across the rocks to where a string of rowboats was cabled and locked to an old piling. These were the same ones she and Becca used to take out to set the crab pots. Even though they were big enough for at least two people, each girl had wanted her own. Becca always chose a red one, while Keely took either a green or blue one.

With her hair whipping across her face, she squatted next to the piling to see if she remembered the combination. It took her three tries, but just as the padlock opened, the sound of gunfire cracked through the night air.

She jumped to her feet and ran to the edge of the beach where Toryn and the others had gone into the forest. She glanced at the *Dee-Light* and saw two dark figures on the bow. Olivia and Sean had heard the gunfire as well.

Her heartbeat thrummed in her ears, drowning out the sound of the wind. She'd nearly gone mad with worry when Vince and Zara finally burst through the trees.

Three young women were huddled between them, none of them Becca. Vince and Zara ushered them over the rocky beach as quickly as they could, considering all of the girls were barefoot. Konal was helping someone else.

"Hanna?" one of the girls in the first group called out.

"I'm right behind you," said the young woman with Konal. She must be the girl from the coffee cart.

When Konal and Hanna got to the water's edge, he gave her his hand and helped her into the dingy like Prince Charming with Cinderella. He turned to leave, but she pleaded for him to stay, so he climbed in and wrapped his arms around her.

"Just for a minute, okay?" Keely heard him say.

She heard a sound on the rocks behind her and she spun around, hoping to see Toryn and Becca, but it was

Asher carrying a woman—not Becca—wrapped burrito-like in a blanket.

Keely scanned the forest, trying to ignore the pit of dread tugging at her stomach.

"Where are Toryn and Becca?" she asked him.

"Toryn is disabling the yacht."

She frowned. "And Becca's with him?"

There was a pained expression on Asher's face, and for a split second, she thought he might be getting ready to tell her something terrible.

"We don't have her yet, but we know where she is," he added hastily. "We needed to get these girls to safety, but Toryn was concerned that Reaux and a few others would escape—with Becca—before we could get back and take them out. They'd barricaded themselves in some sort of underground bunker, and we weren't sure if there were other exits."

The bunkers. Damn. She'd forgotten all about them.

The island had originally been used as a military fort to guard the Puget Sound, but it had been decommissioned many years ago. One of the few remaining vestiges of its original purpose was the underground bunkers.

"So you left Toryn there to disable the yacht's engines on his own?" She felt the anger inside her rising.

"Relax, Keely. He's using his telekinetic Talent from a distance to rip out all the moving parts."

She still didn't like the fact that he was on the other side of the island by himself. In fact, she hated it.

After the girls were safely loaded into the dingy, Asher put a hand on Keely's elbow to help her inside as well, but she stepped away. "That's okay. The boat's too full."

He glanced at the dingy and frowned. "There's plenty of room. Come on."

"No, I'm good. I'll wait." She turned back toward the beach but Asher shot a hand out and stopped her. "What the hell!" she protested. "I'm not leaving without Toryn or my sister."

She tried to jerk away from him, but his grip was like iron.

Toryn almost didn't see them.

He'd been crouching beside one of the seaside cabins, making sure the coast was clear before sprinting toward the dock, when movement to the right caught his attention.

Davin Reaux was emerging from the thick forest, hurriedly escorting a group of people. The wind was strong, but Toryn could hear him. "Come on. Let's go."

Six…seven…eight… Toryn counted them as they hit the beach, recognizing some of them from the video feed at the club. The tenth and final man to come out of the woods was the man who'd been with Becca. And he was leading her by the collar.

Shit. So that's where she'd been. In the bunker with these vile men. He'd searched everywhere in the lodge and cabins for Keely's sister, and when he couldn't find her, he'd feared the worst. She looked cold and scared—the asshole hadn't even given her a coat to wear over that skimpy outfit—but at least she was alive.

He would do whatever it took to get Keely's sister back. He couldn't bear the thought of telling her that he'd seen Becca but hadn't been able to save her. It simply was not an option. There wasn't anything he wouldn't do for the woman he wanted to spend the rest of his life with, including risking his life for her sister.

From what Toryn could tell, there were only two security guards with the group. One on each side. Guns drawn. Heads swiveling, looking for threats. That made ten men total, plus Becca.

Thank the Fates Reaux hadn't brought a large security detail with him to the island. Probably felt it was too remote and thus fairly safe. Or maybe there wasn't room for them on the boat. Whatever the reason, the Iron Guild warriors had taken out most of them in the lodge when they'd rescued the young women.

He shot a glance over his shoulder. Where the hell was his backup? He hadn't disabled the boat yet. If he didn't act now, Reaux would get away and Keely's sister would be gone. Time had officially run out.

He touched the hilt of his knife and considered throwing it. It was a long shot, and he'd have to be deadly accurate. No, Becca was too close. He couldn't take the chance. But even if she weren't and he was lucky enough to hit one of the guards, Reaux would be alerted to his presence. One man against nine, some of them armed, were not good odds.

The group was making its way across the narrow, rocky beach now, heading straight for the tiny marina. Toryn cursed that he hadn't disabled the boat's engines yet. Could he get close enough without them seeing?

Staying low, he sprinted behind the row of cabins to the other side of the cove and stopped inside a thick thatch of trees hanging over the rocky beach. From here, his view of the group was blocked, but the wind brought snippets of their conversation.

"Freezing my nuts off."

"…never to do this again."

"…fun, though, right?"

The boat moored at the end of the dock dwarfed everything around it. Toryn guessed it was close to a hundred feet long. Closing his eyes, he stretched out his mind in the direction of the watercraft, trying to hone in on the engine room, looking for anything mechanical, but he was having trouble finding it.

Damn it. He needed to be closer than this. He was too far away for his Talent to work.

Just as he was about to move, the hairs on the back of his neck prickled and he went for his knife.

"I wouldn't do that if I were you."

He spun around to find a large, bald man pointing a gun at him. Becca's captor.

Toryn didn't wait to find out if the guy was going to shoot or ask questions. Operating on pure instinct, he focused all his kinetic energy on the weapon, and it flew from the man's hands.

Surprise flashed in the large man's eyes before he growled, lowered his head and charged. He wasn't sure if this man was a Shifter-Talent or not, but he certainly looked as if he were capable of shifting into a bear or a bull.

Toryn tried to sidestep out of his way, but his attacker was surprisingly fast and agile for his size. His fist clipped Toryn's shoulder and landed with a dull thud, knocking him to the ground. He jumped to his feet like a cat and palmed his blade.

"You are Iron Guild warrior from Cascadia, yes?" the bald man sneered in an accent Toryn had never heard before. "You do not look so tough to me."

Toryn doubted anyone looked tough to a seven-foot-tall, four-hundred-pound man.

"I went on raid there once. Beautiful women. Brought one back for myself."

"You kidnapped a Cascadian woman?" He'd only

heard of raiding parties taking children. As if that weren't horrible enough.

"Yes, but she not make it. Come home one day and she was dead. Hung herself from neck."

White-hot anger surged through him. This man, and men like him, were exactly why he'd joined the Iron Guild. They came to his world to inflict pain and suffering upon innocent people. But those days were over. Toryn lunged at the guy, slashing and stabbing. This man would never step through a portal and onto Cascadian soil again.

One of Toryn's jabs made contact, slicing across the man's cheek. Seething with rage, the man roared out in pain and charged again.

Toryn stood his ground until the very last second. Stepping to the side, he thrust his blade upward, burying it in the man's abdomen. As the big man's momentum carried him forward, Toryn pulled out his blade and let the body tumble to the rocks below.

A slow clap sounded behind him. "Very nicely done."

Toryn stiffened. But before he could turn around, a sharp pain sliced through his forehead, right between the eyes, and he fell to the ground.

CHAPTER SIXTEEN

Keely clamped a hand over her mouth as she watched Toryn collapse. With his hands clutching his head, he curled into a fetal position and rolled back and forth. He was in agony.

The man with Reaux was a Mind-Talent. She was sure of it. A Mind-Talent could reach into your head and cause excruciating pain. Or worse. They could leave you permanently damaged. She needed to get to Toryn and shield him before it was too late. If it wasn't too late already.

She sprang into action. Asher and Konal would be here any moment. She'd left them to right the dingy that had overturned and thrown all the girls into the icy water of the Puget Sound. They'd be pissed that she left, but she'd deal with their wrath later.

She raced across the beach, almost losing her footing a few times on the rocks and crushed oyster shells.

"Keely? Oh my God." Becca was on the dock, heading toward the large white yacht moored at the end.

Keely didn't hesitate and kept going. Her sister was standing on her own two feet, while Toryn on the other hand was dying. The choice between who needed her most was easy.

She didn't care if anyone in the group had guns or knives. They'd need to be good at hitting a moving target, because she was stopping for no one.

She'd have to get close in order for her Talent to have a chance to work. During their practice sessions, the Grey One had recommended that she have physical contact with the person she was trying to shield. Her Talent wasn't reliable otherwise. She didn't have that luxury now.

She scrambled up the rocky bank where Reaux and another man watched her approach. Toryn was on the ground about twenty feet away with his hands pressed to his temples. Seeing him in pain like this nearly incapacitated her, but she couldn't let herself get distracted. She was here to do a job. Using calming exercises that the Grey One had taught her, she took a deep breath, centered herself and stretched out her mind-shield. Almost instantly she noticed Toryn's shoulders relaxing. And then he stopped writhing. Was it working?

"Well, who do we have here?"

Mr. Reaux was a dark-haired man about the same age as her father, with a bulbous nose and bags under his eyes that indicated he was probably a heavy drinker. The Mind-Talent next to him, a thin, young man, not much older than she was, had a sadistic smile as if he were enjoying himself.

She needed to keep them talking and distracted just long enough for Asher and Konal to get here. Which had to be at any moment.

"I'm Keely Weber. Becca is my sister. You need to let her go." Not that she expected him to do so, but she was trying to buy a little more time.

"Well, well, well. The sister." Reaux looked her up and down, making her feel filthy. "So we have you to thank for the arrival of these barbarians."

Keely gritted her teeth, trying to stay focused on the task at hand. Despite the brisk wind, sweat broke out on her forehead.

"Becca told me all about you. You're the famous Reverend Weber's girls."

Jeez, Becca. What didn't you tell him?

"Yes, that's true," she said while continuing to hold the shield steady. She needed to be careful not to give any indication to the Mind-Talent what she was doing. As far as he knew, he was still having an effect on Toryn.

"Your sister was the one who told us about this place when we decided to move our little soiree off-site. It's surprising what you can learn from an addict. Dangle a couple of pills in front of them, and they'll tell you anything."

It occurred to her that after Reaux found out who Becca was, he'd purposely gotten her using again. A quick Internet search would no doubt turn up all sorts of articles about Reverend Weber's druggie daughter. Reaux had to know it was her Achilles heel.

"One quick call to your father and we ironed out all the details."

Keely's mouth dropped open. She didn't believe it. "My father knows you're here? And he's okay with that?"

"I didn't tell him about your sister, of course. I didn't want to push things too far." Reaux laughed. "Your father is a smart man. He knows you can't have virtue without vice. That's impossible. And when selling virtue makes you a bunch of money, vice becomes even more important."

It felt as if a bomb had been dropped on all she knew to be true, exploding on her past, present and future. Her father, her goddamn father, was involved in this? How was that even possible?

Reaux moved closer. "Let's go." He grabbed her elbow and started to lead her down to the dock.

Something thudded behind them. She turned to see the Mind-Talent crumple to the ground, a knife sticking out of his back. Toryn pulled it out and looked up. Pushing himself to his feet with great effort, his gaze locked onto Reaux's as if he were a shark and the older man was his next meal.

"What the fuck?" Reaux swung her around to use her as an actual shield, but she stumbled over a rock and fell to his feet.

She saw the gun in Reaux's hand and heard the shot a split second before she saw a knife plunge into his chest.

She wheeled around to see Toryn on the ground, blood everywhere.

"Oh my God, no!"

And for the second time tonight, she thought he was dying.

CHAPTER SEVENTEEN

Keely!

Toryn bolted upright but there was only darkness.

Where was she? Was she okay?

Muffled voices, talking gibberish. A weight pressing in on him, forcing him back. Every muscle in his body ached, every damn inch.

Shadows danced on the backs of his eyelids now. Green and blue. It didn't make sense, though. Shadows were supposed to be shades of black and grey.

Keely! Keely!

He couldn't tell if he was screaming out loud or in his head.

He remembered the searing pain in his shoulder, then...

running…

running…

and emptiness.

A festering ball of emptiness in his gut.

He'd been left somewhere cold. Somewhere hurting and alone.

Time passed.

An hour, maybe. A day. A lifetime.

And then he heard a groan. It took him a moment to realize he'd made the sound.

"Hey, man." It was Konal's voice. "You doing okay?"

He cracked open his eyes and saw that he was in his room back at the Iron Haven.

"What happened?" he rasped, his throat dry and parched. "How long have I been out?"

"All night and most of the day. You got shot and a Mind-Talent messed with your head, but you're home now."

Home.

He glanced around the room, expecting to see Keely hovering nearby, but she wasn't here. Nor was there any evidence of her being here either. No chair by the bedside. No book. No knitting project.

"Where's Keely?"

Konal shrugged. "I don't know. Haven't seen her. She didn't come back to the Iron Haven with us."

Didn't come back.

The words rattled in his gut like shards of glass.

"But to be honest with you," Konal continued, "after we got you in the boat and knew you were going to be okay, I didn't pay much attention. Olivia made sure you were healed enough but then had to stop because she was also helping the girls. Hanna was in really bad shape. And Janie—" He shook his head, unable to finish what he was going to say.

Didn't come back.

Those three words haunted him. They'd been the story of his life for as long as he could remember. His mother, then Lucinda, and now Keely? He'd thought she was different. Thought he could trust her, but what the hell did he know?

"So when we got to the marina, she left?" Toryn knew he shouldn't be upset that she'd chosen to be with her sister instead of him. But it wounded his male pride that she left without a word or explanation.

"Yeah," Konal answered.

When he made a move to sit up, a thousand hammers pounded on the inside of his skull. "Bloody hell!"

"No, mate." His friend pushed him back down. "Olivia said you should be resting. In fact, I'm not even supposed to be in here right now. Given what that Mind-Talent did, she said you may feel confused and disorientated at first but that it shouldn't last."

"I'd feel a shit-ton better if this goddamn headache

would stop." A general sense of anger gnawed at Toryn, but he couldn't put his finger on why.

"Oh, I almost forgot." Konal set a bottle of pills on the nightstand next to a glass of water. "Sean said those should help. There aren't many, but he can get more if you need them."

"Fine," he growled. At least his friends cared about him.

After Konal left, Toryn rolled onto his back and stared at the ceiling. Had Keely used him to get what she wanted—just like Lucinda had? Was that it? She didn't need him anymore? Despite her claims, maybe she'd never had any intention of spending her life with a barbarian soldier. He was just a means to an end.

He pushed himself into a sitting position, grabbed the bottle of pills and washed two of them down with a big swig of water.

One thing was certain. He was done acting like a love-struck fool.

Keely stepped through the doors of the Iron Haven, feeling as if a thousand pounds had been lifted from her shoulders. Sean, who'd driven her, was right behind her.

"You're back!" Olivia pushed herself up from where she sat on a sofa in the game room doing a puzzle. She looked tired. Healing people was hard work.

"Oh, don't get up," Keely said. "I just wanted to pop my head in before I head upstairs."

"How did everything go?" Olivia asked, a wary expression on her face.

"Better than I expected, actually. Hard, really hard, but in the end, it was worth it." She swallowed around the lump in her throat. "I'll tell you all about it later. So, how are the patients?"

"Becca is sleeping now," Olivia explained, "but she's doing much better. As are the other girls. Although, I'm afraid, they've got a long way ahead of them."

"Thanks for everything you did to help them. I know it must've taken a lot out of you."

Olivia yawned. "No problem. I'm glad I could help. By the way, Zara said to tell you goodbye. She and Vince headed back to Cascadia this morning. They came over to help with the Iron Havens, but they needed to get back to their son. She really wants you to go over there. I do, too. I think you'd like it."

Warmth blossomed in her chest. It was nice to have female friends who cared about her. "I...I hope I can." She cleared her throat. "So...how's Toryn?"

Olivia gave her a sly smile. "He's a little grumpy."

Keely laughed. "Thanks for the heads-up."

When she got to Toryn's room, she opened the door quietly so as not to disturb him in case he was sleeping.

How strange. The room was empty. She'd figured he would still be in bed, recuperating.

It terrified her how close she'd come to losing him. He'd risked his life to save her sister and those other girls, people he'd never met, all because it was the right thing to do. She let out a slow exhale as the gravity of what he did sank in again. Toryn Flynn literally was her hero.

The whole time she was gone, she'd ached to be by his side, nursing him back to health, but she couldn't for reasons beyond her control. But now she was back and she was here to stay.

She stepped back out into the hallway and saw Sean coming up the stairs. "Do you know where Toryn is?"

"He's not there?"

She shook her head. "I thought for sure he'd be sleeping."

"I heard someone in the garage using a heavy bag. Maybe he's out there talking to one of the guys."

When she got to the garage, she was shocked to see that it wasn't one of the other warriors using the heavy bag, but Toryn.

His injured arm, the right one, was still in a sling, so he was punching the bag with his left hand only. Although it looked like he'd gone through hell and back, he was still as strong and sexy as ever. She couldn't wait to run her hands over his body and reassure herself that he was all right.

"Oh my God, Toryn. What are you doing?" Thanks to Olivia's healing, there were no stitches, but it still couldn't be good for him to be doing such strenuous exercise so soon after being injured.

He didn't even look over. "What does it look like I'm doing?"

Jeez. Olivia was right. He was in a foul mood. Maybe that's what happened when very tough, very strong men became aware that they weren't invincible. They turned into little boys and got pissy. But it made her all the more determined to reinforce his male ego and show him just how strong and capable she thought he was. In the bedroom would be a great place to start.

"I'm so relieved you're feeling better." She stepped in front of the punching bag so he'd have to stop hitting it.

Without even looking at her, he tugged angrily at his sling and grabbed his bottle of water.

She could tell this wasn't going to be easy. "I'm sorry I wasn't here when you woke up. Did you talk to Asher?" She stepped forward, tried to wrap her arms around him, but he pushed her away.

His eyes were dark with anger. "Yeah, I did as a matter of fact. He told me you left as soon as we got back in order to give an interview to that woman. Birdie Lyons."

"Yes, that's true and—"

"I did some checking. She's got the highest ratings among all the news vlogs and is known as the Mouth of the Internet. When you get on Birdie's show, suddenly you're important. But I'm sure you already knew that, didn't you?"

She wasn't liking where this was going. "What are you talking about, Toryn?"

"Fame? Recognition? Sound familiar?"

His words stung as if she'd been struck with a lash. "No," she said. "No, it doesn't."

"Isn't that what your goal was? To get your sister back and become a celebrity? Your father is one. Why not follow in his footsteps? It's in your blood, right? So the first chance you got, you betrayed me."

"Oh my God, Toryn. How could you think that about me? I would never do something to hurt you. And I would never, ever want to be like my father. I thought you knew me well enough by now to know that."

"I'm not stupid, Keely. Facts are facts, and actions speak louder than words. I may have been slow to pick up on the fact that you've been playing me, but not any longer."

Her hand flew to her mouth in horror. Who was this man standing before her? She'd opened up her heart to him, felt more connected to him than any other person on this planet. And now this?

Stunned, she watched as he turned his back on her.

And that was it. He was done talking and had just dismissed her.

She fought back the angry tears stinging her eyes. He didn't even give her the chance to tell him what she'd been talking to Birdie about. He'd straight-up assumed the worst.

Wiping a tear roughly away, she spun on her heel and left. There was no way in hell she was going to let him see just how upset he'd made her.

Toryn was a complete stranger to her, not the man she thought she loved.

CHAPTER EIGHTEEN

Toryn was sitting in a booth at the back of a tavern, nursing his second beer. Keely had been gone for over a week now, and he'd been utterly miserable. He'd been unable to sleep or eat, and the only thing he wanted to do was get shit-faced every day. He didn't want to think about the sad, stricken look on Keely's face right before she left.

He looked up from his glass when Sean slid into the seat across from him. "Thought I'd find you here."

Al's Tavern was the closest pub to the Iron Haven, about thirty miles away. He should've picked a different place. In New Seattle. In the Circus District. Near Sisters Books and Fortunes.

Screw that. She left him. She abandoned him.

"Can't a guy get a little peace and quiet by himself?" he growled.

"Listen, I don't give a shit about you." Sean glared at him from across the table. "It's Rickert. He needs to talk to you."

"What the bloody hell is your problem?" Toryn asked. "Tell Rickert I'll be back when I feel like it." The big man didn't budge. "Go. Leave."

Sean sat back in his seat and folded his muscle-bound arms across his chest like the smug sonofabitch he was. "Look at you," he said, shaking his head, a disgusted look on his face. "You're a self-centered asshole with a perpetual chip on your shoulder. I honestly don't see what she sees in you."

Toryn jumped to his feet. Sean did the same. Damn, he was big. Normally, the guy backed down when Toryn confronted him, but not this time.

"Why?" Toryn seethed. "Are you jealous?"

Sean's punch came lightning fast, catching him on the edge of the jaw. He sprawled backwards and careened into some empty chairs. A few customers gasped.

Sean stood over him, a beast of a man. Legs spread, hands on his hips, he grabbed Toryn by the collar, hauled him to his feet and out into the alley.

"I get that you don't like me," Sean said through clenched teeth once they got outside, away from prying eyes. "And frankly, I really don't give a shit whether you do or not. But for some reason way beyond my comprehension, Keely loves you. She would never betray you. Ever."

"But Birdie—"

"Fuck Birdie Lyons. That gold-digger and her camera crew were at the marina when we got back. They caught wind of what was going on and were waiting for us, ready to go live on the air."

Toryn frowned and rubbed his sore jaw. "But that would've jeopardized all of us."

"Exactly. And Keely knew that. So she made Birdie a deal. Said she'd give her an exclusive interview about her father and what she knew about his involvement with Reaux in exchange for turning off the cameras and not going live with the story until we were gone. And she wanted a chance to tell her mother in person without her hearing about it first on Birdie's show."

"And Birdie agreed?"

"Hell yeah. Turns out Keely's father is with a rival blog network and Birdie has been frothing at the mouth for a chance to take him down."

Toryn leaned back against the brick wall of the alley in shock.

How could he have been so stupid? So blinded by his own fears and wounded pride that he didn't see what he had until it was gone? She wasn't there when he woke up because she'd been protecting them. She'd sacrificed any future chance she might have had to reconcile with her family in order to save him and the rest of the Iron Guild warriors.

Sean was right. He was a fucking asshole. Keely Weber was the best thing that had ever happened to him.

Toryn straightened his jacket. "I've got to go find her. Tell her I'm sorry and beg her to take me back."

Then he looked at Sean as if seeing him for the first time. He was a kind and hardworking man who saw the good in people...even if they didn't deserve it.

"Thank you," Toryn said. "And I'm sorry."

Sean frowned, clearly not believing him. "For what?"

"Thank you for making me see what a jerk I've been. To Keely...and to you." When he got to the door, he turned around. "You're a good man, Sean. And a good friend."

The big man pressed his lips together into a not-quite smile. "Just remember that actions speak louder than any words can."

***

Toryn arrived at Sisters Books and Fortunes to see Verla packing up boxes.

"Where's Keely?" he asked, looking around the empty shop. "Is she upstairs?"

Verla shook her head. "No, she's gone."

"Any idea when she's coming back?"

"She isn't. She and Becca are in Cascadia."

It felt as if he'd been punched again. "What?"

"They left a few days ago. I told her I'd get the rest of the shop packed up for the donation truck. It's coming this afternoon."

"She went there without me?" He stumbled backward, reeling with shock.

He'd wanted to be the one who stepped through the portal with her for the first time. Be there to experience that with her. "But why?"

"Well, if you have to ask," Verla said, rolling her eyes, "then you really are an asshole."

CHAPTER NINETEEN

Keely was in the pasture behind Olivia's mother's cottage, watching a mare and foal kick up their heels in the grass, when she saw a horse and rider approaching. Although she and Becca had been here for almost three weeks, she didn't think she'd ever tire of seeing people using horses as their only mode of transportation.

Becca had accompanied Olivia and her mother, Alexandra, to an open-air market and would be gone all day. Keely had been planning to go, too, but one of the mares was due to foal soon, and Alexandra had asked if she wouldn't mind staying. They'd report back and let her know what they found.

The women were scouting out possible places for the new shop—Sisters Yarns and Fortunes. They didn't have access to books here like they did over on the other side, so they'd have to make do with yarn. But Keely was excited. She loved knitting and crocheting.

The rider rode a majestic horse, a black stallion whose mane and tail were flowing in the wind. As the pair drew near, she realized there was something familiar about the man. The way he carried himself. So tall, so proud.

Her heart raced and her mouth went dry. It was Toryn.

Despite her heartache, there wasn't a day that went by that she didn't miss him. Desperately. If it hadn't been for Becca and her new friends, Neyla, Olivia and Zara, she wouldn't have been able to eat a thing. It made her feel like a selfish idiot to be so down when Becca was the one who'd been through real hell and back.

Toryn reined in the horse beside her.

"You found me," she said. It occurred to her that Becca, Olivia and Alexandra may have known about this.

"Aye, I did. We have unfinished business to attend to." He reached his hand down to pull her up behind him, but she took a step backward.

"If you want to talk, we can do it here," she said, crossing her arms over her chest. A man couldn't be a complete and utter asshole and then think he could just ride in and sweep a woman off her feet.

"Please, Kitten. Will ye come with me? There's something I'd like to show ye."

She sighed. That nickname. It got her every single time. Okay, fine. She'd go.

She held out her hand and he pulled her up behind him. Wrapping her arms around his waist, she pressed her cheek to his back and inhaled. She'd really missed how he smelled.

They galloped down through a narrow basin and into a cottonwood forest. Then he reined in the horse at the edge of a bluff. The view was stunning with craggy mountains all around them.

He dismounted, then reached up and helped her down.

"So what's this all about?" she asked.

"A good friend told me that actions speak louder than words, so I wanted to show you something…while I grovel for forgiveness."

He led her to a semi-circle of large rocks, protected from the winds. He opened up a pack and in a few minutes, he'd laid out a gourmet meal of cheeses, fruits, various meats and breads, along with a jug of what appeared to be wine and a bouquet of wildflowers.

He sat her down on the blanket and took her hands in his. "First of all, I want to apologize for the way I spoke to you. I was a colossal jerk and can't believe what I said. It was wrong of me, rude and horrible."

"Yes, it was. You hurt me, Toryn. Terribly."

"I know." Regret tightened the corners of his mouth.

"And if I have to spend the rest of my life making it up to you, I will."

"Okay, maybe that's taking things a little *too* far. I mean you were injured, not yourself."

His jaw ticked. "That's still not an excuse. I allowed my fears of abandonment and betrayal to color my viewpoint, which prevented me from seeing the amazing woman I had in front of me. I'm done living in the past now. I'm tired of that yoke around my neck."

She caressed his cheek. "I understand all too well how difficult it is to live with past hurts. They affect everything."

He leaned into her hand, his eyes sparkling with emotion. "I want to live for now and for the future. I want to live for us." Then he reached into his pocket and pulled out a small book.

She took one look at it and gasped. "Is that…is that mine?"

"Aye. I went to the shop and saw it in one of your boxes to be donated. It's one of your favorites, isn't it? The one with the poetry you have tattooed on your arm?"

She nodded, tears stinging the backs of her eyes. "But how did you get it through the portal? Everything disintegrates when you cross over."

"Not dense metal objects or items *inside* a dense metal object."

"But what about the portal sickness?"

He gave her a wry smile. "I've been in Cascadia for almost three weeks. I came over a few days after you."

"And you've been sick the whole time?"

He nodded. "Olivia offered to heal me, but I wouldn't let her."

Keely's eyes widened. "Olivia? She knew you were here?"

"I made her swear she wouldn't tell you. But I'm feeling better now. A whole lot better. I'd do anything for you, Keely, *anything*. But—"

"But what?"

He took a deep breath, let it out slowly. "Can you ever forgive me?"

"Oh, Toryn, I already have."

His fingers grazed her jaw tenderly, then he cupped the back of her neck and drew her close. His kiss was gentle at first but quickly turned hungry. When you needed someone as much as the air you breathed, three weeks was an awful long time to be apart. Her nipples tingled and the juncture between her thighs ached with anticipation as they tore off their clothes.

His gaze darkened with desire as it swept over her naked body. "Ye are so beautiful, Kitten. I want to lick every inch of you."

"Then what's stopping you?" she breathed wickedly.

His lips twisted. "Not a damn thing. I just wanted ye to know my intentions."

He pushed her down on the blankets and spread her

knees apart. A low growl came from his throat as he dipped his head between her legs. She would never, not in a million years, grow tired of his desire for her.

He licked the seam of her sex in one achingly slow motion that had her crying out his name even before he suckled her clit between his teeth. She gripped handfuls of his hair and held on tight as waves of pleasure spiraled through her body, igniting every nerve ending and turning her bones to rubber. Just as she was about to shatter, he broke away, pulled himself on top of her and slipped the head of his cock between her folds. She was so wet that he easily slid inside. Her inner muscles clenched around him.

"Oh, God, Toryn…I'm…having another one." She gave a strangled cry as another orgasm slammed through her.

He pushed himself up on his elbows, increasing his tempo until his whole body went rigid. Groaning loudly, he arched his head back, the cords in his neck straining.

God he was beautiful, she thought, still in the throes of her own pleasure. *And he's all mine.*

After it was all over and they were cuddling under the blankets, Toryn rolled onto his side to face her. Tendrils of his dark hair fell over his sweaty forehead. He looked completely sated.

She smiled to herself, feeling even more satisfied. *I did that to him,* she thought proudly.

"Keely," he said, his broad, warm hand splayed across

her belly, "you're the best thing that ever happened to me. I want to be your man, through good times and in bad. I don't ever want to be away from ye again." He cleared his throat, his voice rough with emotion. "These last three weeks were some of the worst in my life."

"Mine, too," she admitted.

"Kitten, will ye marry me? Will ye make this man—this, imperfect man—whole again? Please say yes. Make me the happiest man in the world—two worlds."

She held his face in her hands and kissed his lips. "Oh Toryn, I love you. My answer is yes."

Hope you enjoyed *Heartless Rebel* as much as I enjoyed writing it!

Please consider leaving a review at your favorite online retailer and/or Goodreads to help the series grow. Even if it's just a line or two, honest reviews help other readers decide if they'd like the books too.

Have you read the other books in the Iron Portal series yet?

Sign up for my VIP reader list to be the first to know about new releases, sales, freebies and other fun goodies!

http://laurielondonbooks.com/mailing-list-sign-up/

Keep reading for an excerpt of **Bonded By Blood**, book 1 in the sexy and dangerous Sweetblood series. Inspired by my obsession with vampires, it's the book that started it all!

EXCERPT FROM BONDED BY BLOOD

Some cravings are too powerful to resist...

Movie location scout Mackenzie Foster-Shaw has always known that she's cursed to die young. No one can protect her from the evil that has stalked her family for generations—vampires who crave her rare blood type. Until one afternoon in a wooded cemetery, she encounters an impossibly sexy stranger, a man she must trust with her life.

For Dominic, a man haunted by loss, Mackenzie satisfies a primal hunger that torments him—and the bond they share goes beyond heat, beyond love. She alone can supply the strength he needs to claim his revenge. But in doing so, he could destroy her...

Mackenzie Foster-Shaw spotted the cemetery sign the last minute and squeezed the brakes, spinning out her white Triumph motorcycle in a spray of dirt and gravel. She'd meant to lean into a sharp, controlled turn, but the back tire lost traction and she almost had to lay the thing down.

Crap, the rocks hadn't looked that loose.

Irritation her carelessness momentarily replaced the uncertain riding in with her as she sprang from the bike. After examining the chrome for chips and seeing no damage, she felt the hard lump of anticipation return, but she swallowed and tried to ignore it.

She yanked off her helmet and squinted into the shadowed interior of the cemetery. Even in the late afternoon sun, little light penetrated the heavy canopy of fir trees.

"I'm liking this so far," she said to herself as she tossed her sunglasses on the seat. But she knew better than get her hopes up too soon. Hope didn't pay the bills, nor did wishful thinking.

Situated on a forest access road, miles from the main highway, the cemetery was certainly ancient enough. The county register listed it as one of the oldest in the region. How long had it been since anyone visited this place? Ages ago, probably.

She started to unzip her leather jacket, then hesitated.

Like most people in the Pacific Northwest after

months of gray skies and the unending wetness of winter, she didn't need much of an excuse to strip off the layers. But with one glance at the bushes she'd need to traipse through, she zipped it back up. Those vivid green leaves couldn't camouflage the barb-covered vines eager to hook anything within reach. Especially bare skin. Besides, it was probably cooler and wetter inside the trees.

She grabbed her camera from the saddlebag and fiddled with the settings, not bothering with the flash attachment. The client was adamant the pictures needed to portray the ambient lighting and convey an oppressive, haunted feeling.

"Hopefully, *this* location will work for them." It was the fourth or fifth graveyard she'd visited in the past two weeks. If it didn't, she was screwed because she was totally out of ideas.

Bear Creek Pioneer Cemetery was etched in once-white paint on a crooked sign at the side of the road. After shooting a few pictures, she scanned the area for a pathway and noticed a slight indentation in the underbrush. She'd do her sketches and take measurements of the road later.

Her boots crunched on the gravel as she slung the camera strap over her shoulder and plunged into the blackberry bushes. Good thing she'd kept her riding leathers on. Both the jacket and the pants. Sharp thorns and stickers grabbed hungrily at her arms and legs, but they weren't able to gain purchase on the thick hide.

As she stepped into the small clearing, the still, dank air clung to her face. Tufts of tangled grasses crowded around the crumbling headstones in the middle of the cemetery, but at the edge, the bushes covered them completely.

Oppressive? Most definitely.

Her stomach lurched with excitement, but again, she quickly tamped it down and got to work.

Opening the tripod, she balanced it on the uneven ground next to a stone cross. Something about it made her hesitate. The name was no longer legible and she paused to run a finger over the weathered, rough surface. Who was buried here, gone and forgotten? A man? A woman? A child?

She must have stared a little too long because her sinuses began to itch. She wrinkled her nose, tried to sniff away the sudden heavy weight pulling at her heart, but it didn't quite work.

Would someone wonder about her, too? What she looked like. What kind of a person she was. How long from now? Months? Years, maybe? If she were lucky. But the thing was, there'd be no body in her grave.

Stop. Just stop it. Quit being so damn morbid.

Normally she was pretty good at not thinking much about the future. Why worry about something completely out of her control? It had to be all these depressing cemeteries she'd been visiting lately.

She took a deep breath to change the unproductive air in her lungs, screwed the camera in place and exhaled, wrenching her mind back to the present where it needed to stay.

With every satisfying click of the shutter, the outside world became only what she could see through the viewfinder. The gravestones, the trees and the quiet loneliness.

When she finally stopped to examine the results, her pulse jumped like it always did when she captured something magical through the lens. They were good. Really good. Much better than the other locations.

She hesitated when she got one particular image. The lengthening shadows stretched out over the headstones and mounds of grass like the distorted, tortured lines of Munch's painting, *The Scream*, and her spine prickled.

Or maybe it was the wind.

A slight breeze found its way into the open collar of her jacket, tickling her neck and ears, and stirring the branches of the watchful trees. She shivered and brushed her hair away from the lens.

Zombies? Dead eyes and insatiable cravings? She could totally visualize rotting hands stretching out of their graves here. Would Hollywood think so? That was the fifteen hundred dollar bonus question.

She twisted her hair up, clipped it off her neck, and dropped to the forest floor. Although it hadn't rained, moisture lingered everywhere and the ground smelled woodsy beneath her. She rolled over onto her back, again thankful she'd decided to keep the jacket on. A few wispy fronds of grass brushed her cheek and she batted them way. Twisting the lens to focus on the treetops, she—

A sound sliced through the silence of the graveyard and she froze.

A cry? A growl?

She patted her jacket pocket and felt the reassuring hard lump of her handgun.

Maybe it was just the squeak of tree limbs protesting against the wind. Of course, it was. With shaking hands, she pushed herself to a sitting position just to make sure.

When she heard it again, she scrambled to her feet.

An animal. Definitely not a tree limb.

She held her breath and fixated on the spot at the edge of the cemetery where the noise originated.

A mound of leaves and branches moved. Twenty feet or so in front of her.

Her pulse thundered behind her eardrums. It was probably just a raccoon. But didn't they hiss? She took a step backwards, her gaze unwavering.

A badger? They were mean sons of bitches. No, this definitely didn't sound like the one that crawled into their tent on the last camping trip with her father all those years ago. This sounded bigger, different.

Her breath came out in shallow bursts as she glanced behind her. Okay. Her bike was about thirty steps away then up that slight embankment through the sticker bushes. If she ran, would the thing chase her? If she moved slowly, would it even follow? No, it was probably even more scared of her. She eased the camera strap around her neck and—

She heard it again.

This time it was unmistakable.

"Help me."

The pile of leaves shuffled, falling away to reveal a man hidden underneath. With a hand outstretched to her, he writhed as if in pain.

A man? What the hell? Here in the middle of nowhere? Should she run for help? Should she walk closer?

Even from this distance, she could see his brow furrowed in agony, his eyes desperate and hollow. He didn't appear to be in any shape to harm her. Besides, she had her gun.

Recalling her mother's stern warnings over the years, she paused. This couldn't have anything to do with her family, could it?

Her cousin Stacy's face flashed in her memory along with the faded one of her father. But this wasn't the big city, nor was it summer. Two critical elements. Usually.

She placed a cool hand to her throat, the racing tempo of her heart slowed just a little, and she considered her options. Maybe this was his version of "here little girl, help me with my puppy." Clear out here though? It wasn't like this place got a lot of foot traffic.

He dropped his arm and his mouth moved silently. God, he really seemed hurt. She had to do something; she couldn't just leave him.

She pulled out her cell phone, punched 911, and kept a finger above Send. Shaking off myriad notions of zombies and cemeteries, she strode forward to the edge of the trees.

The man lay on his back, half-hidden under the leaves and branches, his clothes covered in dirt. Given his disheveled appearance, he looked like a vagrant. But then she noted his expensive-looking boots and pale blue dress shirt, and he, too, was wearing leather pants. Most definitely not homeless.

Torn and muddy, his shirt was unbuttoned, ripped open actually, revealing a dirt-smeared but well-defined chest. Some of his shoulder-length dark hair, tangled with bits of leaves and debris, seemed to be partially captured in a ponytail, but she couldn't be sure from this angle. His eyes, an electrifying shade of ice blue, pierced through her. She stopped a few feet away.

"What happened to you? Are you hurt?"

"I need...your help." His voice, slightly accented, was clearly laced with pain.

At that moment, the wind picked up and swirled at her feet as if urging her to move. The leaves around him danced on the air and settled slowly back to the ground. Stepping closer, she heard his sharp intake of breath. His eyes widened at first then narrowed to slits, and he shrank backwards into the leaves.

He couldn't be scared of her, could he? He was a tall man, athletic and powerfully built. Why would he be afraid of her?

"Stay away," he ordered. Given his condition, his forceful tone surprised her.

She didn't understand. Why the sudden turnabout? He clearly needed her help. He had to be hallucinating. How long had he been here anyway? Squatting down to appear less intimidating, she tucked her phone in her pocket and stretched out her hands like she would to a frightened dog. "It's okay. I won't hurt you. I can help."

Then she saw it. A hole in his mud-encrusted shirt. She hadn't noticed it right away because it was fairly small, the size of a quarter maybe, and he cradled his arm as if it were injured.

"Oh my God. Is that...blood? Have you been shot?"

As she sprang to his side, the last thing she remembered was the way his pupils suddenly dilated. Like a shark rolling back its eyes when it bites.

ALSO BY LAURIE LONDON

Iron Portal Series

DARK ASSASSIN

MIDNIGHT ROGUE

HIDDEN WARRIOR

HEARTLESS REBEL

Sweetblood Series

BONDED BY BLOOD

EMBRACED BY BLOOD

TEMPTED BY BLOOD

SEDUCED BY BLOOD

HIDDEN BY BLOOD

ENCHANTED BY BLOOD

ENTICED BY BLOOD

UNRAVELED BY BLOOD

Nocturne Falls Universe

HOW KNOT TO MARRY A VAMPIRE

ABOUT THE AUTHOR

Laurie London is the bestselling author of the Sweetblood and Iron Portal series—dark, sexy paranormal romance, set primarily in the Pacific Northwest. Publisher's Weekly has called her work "sexy" and "sizzling."

Laurie lives on a small town outside of Seattle with her family. Armed with a business degree, she worked for a Fortune 500 company in IT and as an underwriter. After a hiatus to raise two children and a variety of animals, she studied, apprenticed for and became a licensed optician. Her other jobs included cocktail waitress, hotel maid, candy store manager and bridal gown sales, so she is well qualified to be a writer.

Find Laurie online:
www.LaurieLondonBooks.com